Tales From the Empty Notebook

Tales From The Empty Notebook

William Kotzwinkle
Illustrations by Joe Servello

MARLOWE & COMPANY
NEW YORK

First Edition

Published by
Marlowe & Company
632 Broadway, Seventh Floor
New York NY 10012

http://www.marlowepub.com

Copyright © 1996 by William Kotzwinkle
Illustrations copyright © 1996 by Joe Servello
Text design by Felice Ponger, Neuwirth & Associates, Inc.

Library of Congress Catalogue Card Number 96-76837

Manufactured in the United States of America.

ISBN 1-56924-786-2 (paper)
ISBN 1-56924-792-7 (cloth)

Contents

"nd does anyone ever go into Uncle's old study?" I looked up the stairs, toward the old, dark cyprus door.

"Not often," said my cousin, who had recently become the new master of the house. "It has a melancholy air about it."

"Uncle wasn't happy there? I thought he spent all his time in that study."

"For the last ten years of his life he hardly budged from it," said my cousin. "He was supposed to have been writing stories, you see. But after he died, and we went in to straighten the place up, we found that all his notebooks were empty." My cousin looked at me. "He'd never written a word."

I continued staring at the door, and thinking about what the hours must have been like for my poor uncle, up there, pretending to write, and having nothing at all to show for ten full years of his life.

"Whenever we asked him how his stories were coming," said my cousin, "he always told us how marvelous they were, and became very excited. The stories, he said, were popping out of his head so fast, he could hardly keep up with them. Well, he was a dreamer, you see, and his stories were just a dream, too. You can look for yourself after supper. I'll have the fire lit in there, and you can see his notebooks for yourself. You won't find so much as a pen stroke in a single one of them."

I took my cousin at his word, and following supper, I entered through the old cyprus doorway, into Uncle's study. As promised, a fire was crackling in the fireplace, and the lamps had been lit. The desk was large, made of finely polished oak, and Uncle's chair was of a thick leather, with many creases and wrinkles upon it, from much use.

A pen rested in its onyx holder, and a bottle of ink stood beside it. Lifting the bottle to the light, I saw that it was full. Not one drop had ever touched paper.

Poor Uncle! I could feel how great his torment must have been, to be in here, with the other members of the household waiting for that wonderful day when he would seat them around the living room, and read to them something of his own creation.

Was the air melancholy, as my cousin had said? I felt, rather, a cloud of ideas, hovering still, like a thunderstorm which had never burst. Yes, the air was thick, as if filled with some strange atmospheric pressure, but one which a barometer could not measure, only the human heart.

I stirred the fire, then sat myself down in Uncle's chair. The aroma of his tobacco had gotten into things, into the walls and the carpet. It was a pleasant smell, so faint, faint as a spirit. How often the bluish smoke from his pipe must have hung over this lamp, and swirled, and made him dream. And how he must have longed to realize those dreams. And picked up his pen. And thought, Now I'll begin.

Looking around his study, I saw that the walls were lined with the books of the great storytellers of the ages—old leather bindings fine-tooled in gold, and bearing the names of immortal works of the imagination. Here was his inspiration, and here, I'm sure, were his dearest friends, those figures who live in tales.

But he'd had another friend, for the edges of the leather chair were covered with claw marks, such as a cat makes when she is contemplating a leap into one's lap. Yes, here Uncle had sat, with puss in his arms, adding her dreams to his own. He'd stroked her soft fur, and whispered many secrets to her, perhaps his darkest secret of all, that his notebooks were empty. But puss wouldn't have minded, for cats keep their own tale well hidden.

Upon the shelf directly beside the desk, was a row

of notebooks, each one well-bound. I imagined Uncle taking down one of these notebooks each morning and replacing it at bedtime, untouched by his pen. These were his collected works—blank pages—which rested alongside the gold-tooled volumes of the masters, whose pages were full.

Yes, it was pathetic to see his empty notebooks ranked beside the great works, and I suppose I began to feel something of what my cousin felt—a melancholy despair. But just then, the fire in the fireplace made a loud popping noise, and as the logs fell into the center of the grate, a brilliant tongue of flame rose up, and cast a host of dancing shadows in the study.

And I had the oddest urge to take down one of the notebooks.

I gripped the spine of the first of them. As I did so, it seemed as if my arm were that of another. The fire flared up again; I brought the notebook to the desk, and opened it.

The page was, of course, empty.

But my eyes seemed to go out of focus, as when one is peering intently through the fog, trying to make out some distant object; the fog dances, and tantalizing forms take shape.

So now with the page before me; it seemed like fog, with shapes inside it. I rubbed my eyes and the fog was gone, but in its place there was a faint script forming on the page—of the palest blue imaginable. I could barely make it out, but I knew what I must do. I opened Uncle's inkwell, and took up his pen in my hand.

I worked fully through the night, tracing with ink the ghostly script appearing on the page before me. They were my Uncle's stories—the dreams he dreamt but could not write in life. Somehow, in the world beyond our own, he'd finally set them down.

First Tale
From the Empty Notebook

Penman's Paradise

"For the best ink, you must gather rainwater. Is there any among you bright enough to do that?"

"Yes sir," said the penman's students, ringed around him with their copy books in hand.

"And to thin it—vinegar. Water will dim the ink, but vinegar will allow it to keep its brightness." The penman looked at his pupils, and knew that not one of them yet comprehended the great adventure that lay ahead.

"If you are caught on some battlefield, and you have lost your ink, and yet must write a message to be posted to the king's general far hence—cut off a piece of your wool robe, and set fire to it."

"Fire, sir? But where's the ink from that, sir?"

"The black soot, my little dunces. Mix with rain-water, thin with vinegar, and you shall have ink to send your king's message."

The penman handed round a number of sheets on which his own pure penmanship flowed, but in a faint blue ink, so faint as to hardly be seen at all. "Now, each of you, trace with your pen what my pen has done."

His pupils wrote with shaky hands, but time, he knew, would change that. In months to come, they'd begin to learn the secret of the art, and then the secret of the secret, and then the deeper secret still, and finally they would enter the Fair Hand's Labyrinth.

The hour passed, the lesson concluding with advice on choosing a quill. "It must come from a goose, but not just any goose. It must be a Dutch or Italian goose. And it must not be just any feather from such a goose, but the third or fourth left wing feather, for then its point will curve to the right, and the enchanted figures will more readily appear."

"Enchanted, sir?"

"Yes, enchanted." He held up his inkwell, made of a hollow stag's horn. "You see here a lake, my young friends, in which mysterious creatures live. They swim in its depths, and your pen is the pole by which you go fishing. Some day you shall catch a dragon. Or a faun playing on his pipes. For they all live inside the black lake."

He dipped his fine quill into the ink, and laid his pen to a piece of white parchment. In a few strokes, the penmaster's hand produced letters of the most decorative sort, embroidered with vines and flowers.

"Indeed, sir, you've got something on your line!"

"So I have, my young friends. Now watch its mirror image appear." And he drew a second set of decorative letters, facing in the opposite direction.

"The master writes backwards!"

He laid his pen down and smiled at them. He had them now, had them caught on his line as if they were what he'd been fishing for. They'd study, and they'd return to his studio, to learn more. And one day, their writing would have proportion and swiftness.

"Very well, my little nibs, you may go. Class dismissed until tomorrow."

The penman retired to his private study. The day was ending, and shadows falling across his work table. His cat awoke, on her cushion by the window; she arched her back, and came purring to the penman. He picked her up, and cradled her in his arms, and together they watched the setting sun. "And did you chase mice in your dreams? Or were you a leopard while you slept? I shall never know, shall I?"

He scratched her on her furrowed brow, and she rubbed her whiskered cheek against his portly stomach, for the penman was a rather stout fellow, given to enjoying the good things of life, like fine food and comfortable chairs. His cat agreed entirely with this philosophy. He heated some milk for her, which she liked before supper. And for himself he had a glass of mulled wine, and some cheese.

"Just a snack, to whet our appetites, eh, my pretty

whiskered friend? And in a little while, we'll have some kidney pie."

The cat looked up from her bowl of milk, and her loud purr seemed to say that, yes, kidney pie sounded fine.

The penman settled in at his desk, lighting the lamp and uncovering his ink. His cat leapt up onto the desk and settled down beside him, to wash her white paws; she never disturbed paper or ink, for a penman's cat must be well behaved. The penman unrolled his parchment, dipped his quill into the ink, and from the tip of his quill fabulous beasts began to flow, parading among the letters of the alphabet.

He wrote, and the cat washed, the two working side by side, but the cat tired first, sighed a deep sigh, and went to sleep, while the penman kept at his bestiary of the fantastic. His big belly rested against the edge of the desk, and he muttered in a deep, gravelly voice, ". . . roundness and slope . . . and a lively stroke . . . just a few letters more and then we shall eat . . ."

But he worked on, at another letter and another, joining them in graceful sequence. His cat twitched in her sleep, and the penman's supper was forgotten, and it was on the tail of a flying reptile that he encountered the doorway to Penman's Paradise.

He'd made the tail become a whorl of ink, his pen going in swift circles. At some point in the whorl, he realized his arm was possessed. He could not stop its movement; his wrist was spinning, round and round, the ink was flowing, down and down, and he was following after it, into a dark whirling pool.

He saw only black, the deepest richest black he'd ever known, blacker than any ink he'd ever mixed of gallnut, gum, and nitre. He spun through it, arms outstretched, unable to stop himself.

He seemed to fall for ages, down the long spout of the whirlpool, until he tasted vinegar. "The ink is beginning to thin," he muttered, and observed his words coming out of his mouth written on a paper scroll.

The ink continued to thin, then vanished completely, and he was deposited, very lightly for one of such corpulence, upon a vast plain of parchment. At the horizon, the edges of the parchment curled up, and in the sky floated clouds of silk, such as scribes use to cover their inkwells.

Across the plain, an extraordinary figure came— its body made of curlicues and flourishes. It was a centaur, half-man, half-horse, and obviously drawn by a master penman, for its horns had exquisite little points, its hooves were finely pointed too, and its delicate limbs were all perfectly proportioned.

"Good evening," said the centaur, its words, like the penman's, coming out on a little lettered scroll that floated momentarily in the air, and then disappeared.

A moment later, a curlicued dog showed up, then a pony, and finally a monkey—each one made from single, unbroken lines that shaped their odd anatomy.

"Where am I?" asked the penman.

"You're in Penman's Paradise," said the animals in unison, little scrolls coming from each of their mouths.

"I'm terribly confused," said the penman. "I've

missed my kidney pie, and when that happens I always feel a little weak."

"Well, draw up a chair and sit down," said the little monkey, its curlicued tail whipping back and forth.

"But there is no chair here," said the penman.

The monkey curled its tail around, pointing it at the penman's hand, which still clutched his goose quill.

"Ah, you mean *draw* a chair," said the penman.

"Or draw *up* a chair," said the monkey. "I see no great difference."

"No," said the penman, "I don't suppose a monkey would." But he took out a little vial of ink which he always kept on a chain around his neck, and opened it up; then into it he dipped his quill and made a few quick strokes in the air; the point of his pen was met by a subtle substance, which gave shape to a perfectly suitable chair, and on it the penman sat, with the animals around him.

"Is there anything *else* you need?" asked the monkey, rather impatiently.

"As I say, I've missed my supper."

"I see," said the monkey, exasperatedly. "Well, you are slow-witted, aren't you."

"And why are you such an impatient animal?" asked the penman.

"I'm not impatient. I'm beautiful," said the monkey, and turned around, displaying the perfect symmetry of its form. "And you can eat anytime you like." It pointed its elegant tail once again at the penman's quill.

"Oh . . . oh, yes, I see . . ." The penman drew himself

a nice long loaf of bread, which, though it was black as ink and tasted a little vinegary, was quite satisfying. "And now," he said, "perhaps I should be going. For though I have eaten, my cat has not."

But before he'd even gotten to his feet, the animals bolted in fear, for a monstrous creature had appeared on the horizon—a horrible bird whose huge beak was cutting through the parchment land.

"Scissor Beak!" cried the animals.

The penman leapt to his feet, as the huge glinting blades of a gigantic shears sliced toward him.

"Dear me," he said, and lifting up the ends of his scholar's robe, he followed the animals in their flight. They ran much faster than he could, their fine, light limbs bending and unbending gracefully. The penman struggled along, and the words *huff* and *puff* came out of his lips on two short little scrolls, and then fell behind him, where they were cut neatly in half by the swiftly moving shears.

The animals had already vanished over some far edge of the parchment, and the penman, holding stomach in one hand and the hem of his robe in the other, looked around in despair for some place to hide.

This way

popped out on a scroll, from a trapdoor cut in the parchment floor. The penman jumped down into it, and was greeted by a poorly drawn, hunched little faun, whose limbs were not well connected at all.

"What a mess you are," said the penman.

"We'll be in a bigger mess if Scissor Beak gets us," said the little faun, and he grabbed the penman's hand in his own and yanked him out of the way, as the huge glinting point of the shears flashed just beside them. The penman fell backward in terror, and the little faun tugged at his robe, and led him up another flight of steps, to a second trapdoor, out of which they popped.

"There," said the faun, pointing with a twisted arm. The giant shears had gone by, cutting off into the distance.

"How distressing," said the penman. "Does the Scissor Beak come through often?"

"Once a day," said the faun. "You get used to it."

"But what if you were sleeping, or looking the other way!"

"Then half of you would be here and the other half would wind up—" The faun pointed toward the cliff that had just been formed by the Scissor Beak cutting through the land.

"Dreadful," said the penman.

"Definitely," said the faun, and led him over to the cliff edge. "Look down there," said the faun.

The penman was not especially fond of heights, and he approached cautiously, still holding up the hem of his robe. Peeking over the edge, he saw the top of a magnificent forest, whose azure, gold, and vermillion branches were filled with every manner of fabulous being.

"I must get closer," he said, and went so far as to kneel on the flimsy edge of the parchment, which sagged ominously.

The faun nodded, and gave a loud whistle. A moment later, there was a labored beating of wings, and a poorly drawn, cockeyed flying dragon appeared in the sky overhead. The dragon circled uncertainly a few times, and then attempted a landing. Its crooked wings beat and flapped, its twisted claws scratched desperately, and it hit the ground in a sprawling tumble, rolling end over end.

". . . confounded wings . . . never work properly . . ." The dragon came to a stop a few yards away, picked itself up, and attempted a jaunty manner. "How may I be of assistance?"

"We want you to fly us down there," said the faun.

"Certainly," said the dragon. "Nothing easier."

The penman and the faun climbed on the dragon's back. It curled its long neck around and looked at them with its cross-eyes. "Keep properly balanced. Most important."

It waddled slowly away from the cliff edge, turned, took a few deep breaths, and then started to run toward the cliff edge, its scrawny, misshapen wings beating at the air.

The penman desperately grabbed the dragon's long skinny neck.

"I say . . ." gasped the dragon. ". . . this is hard enough . . . without being strangled . . ."

The dragon leapt into the air, and they sailed off the edge of the cliff. ". . . balance . . . proper balance . . ." The dragon pitched over, wings flapping wildly.

The penman leaned to the other side, and the dragon came upright again. "That's better," it said, and went into a slow turn, but a second later it pitched to the other side, and the penman found

18

himself hanging upside-down in the air, his robe up over his head.

He stared in terror at the forest spiraling beneath them. The dragon craned its neck back around toward its passengers. "Landing should be quite simple."

Saying so, the cross-eyed creature folded its wings and went into a dive. The penman saw a clearing in the illuminated trees, which held a golden meadow, and a shining lake. The dragon spread its wings for a landing in the meadow, and they came down in the lake.

"Terribly sorry," said the creature, as they sank into the depths. Its word-scroll came out underwater, in a soggy limp mess whose ink ran badly. *Misjudged the altitude . . . cross-eyed, you know.*

The penman's heavy robe held him underwater, and the faun had to shove him up to the surface, where a little scroll saying *gasp sputter* flopped soggily out of the penman's mouth.

The three fliers crawled to shore, and the penman looked at the dragon. "I don't wish to insult you, but whoever drew your wings should be made to fly with you."

The penman wrung out the end of his robe. He had no more time to think about distorted dragons, for the illuminated forest was before him—a forest of magnificent capital letters, with thick trunks below and twisting, gnarled branches above. He entered into the shaded corridors formed by the letters, and the little faun limped along beside him. "We mustn't stray too far inside."

But the penman continued on, enraptured by the illuminated colors, which led him deeper and deeper.

The cross-eyed dragon tagged along behind, preening its raggedy feathers. "I like to keep myself looking well. A point of pride, don't you see . . ."

Golden monkeys swung in the golden trees, eating blue apples. Dewdrops sparkled on the leaves, and when the branches shook the penman saw that the dewdrops were tiny diamonds.

"I don't say I'm a perfect flier, no." The dragon was marching along behind the penman. "I have slight technical problems in the tail. But all in all, I think I do rather well."

"Yes, you do," said the penman. "You're the picture of grace in the air."

"How kind of you to say so," said the dragon.

The limping faun turned to the dragon. "You maneuver like a swallow. You're as light as a hummingbird."

"Oh, I *say*," said the cross-eyed dragon, and its neck feathers puffed up proudly.

"Excuse me," said the penman, "but what is that large creature just ahead, the one that seems to be charging directly at us?"

"It's the Gumma!" cried the faun.

"Quick!" commanded the dragon, bending over, and the penman and the faun leapt on its back.

The animal thundered toward them through the forest corridor, on legs so tiny they couldn't be seen, its great, gray bulk pushing forward with a shuddering motion. The grass beneath it vanished, the leaves in its path were gobbled up, and as it skidded sideways, a monkey lost its tail.

"Horrible, awful Gumma!" shouted the monkey, waving its fist and throwing a blue apple at the Gumma, which simply devoured it in its round, mouthless snout.

". . . trying to get off the ground here . . . spot of difficulty . . ." The cross-eyed dragon was madly flapping its clumsy wings; the penman turned and saw the Gumma only a few feet behind them.

"We're going to be rubbed out!" cried the faun.

". . . wings beating . . . tail feathers spread . . . what have I forgotten . . ."

The penman reached into his robe. "We must call on the power of the pen." Saying so, he brought out a sharply pointed metal nib, and stuck the dragon in the rear with it.

The dragon's bent beak opened in a screech, and it leapt into the air. Its flapping wings caught the wind and it sailed upward, as the charging Gumma passed directly beneath. The dragon craned its neck around quickly, looking both ways. ". . . circling nicely now . . ."

It banged into a tree trunk, and spilled penman and faun into the branches, where they grabbed onto a gnarled vine and clung there, as the horrible Gumma shuddered on out of sight.

The dragon beat the air in front of them, wings working frantically. "Light as a hummingbird, eh? Wouldn't you say? The way I took off from a dead stop?"

"Yes," said the penman, "you did very well."

The dragon landed on a branch just below them,

and wobbled there, steadying itself. ". . . balance is everything . . . I have a knack for it . . ."

The penman examined his robe, which had been torn in the crash. It was also wet, and most uncomfortable. "I think I should return to my studio." He looked at the little faun. "Do you have any suggestions?"

"There's only one way out," said the faun.

"And that is?"

"Through the Fair Hand's Labyrinth." The faun pointed with a crooked finger. "It is somewhere beyond this forest."

They climbed down out of the tree, and the tailless monkey scrambled over to them. "Penman," it said. "Can you draw me a new tail?"

"Certainly," said the penman, and took out his quill and ink. "Bend over, please."

The monkey bent over, and the penman, with one easy flourish, restored the creature's tail. "How pretty!" cried the monkey, admiring its loop.

The penman looked at his two other companions. "Why don't I correct all the mistakes that trouble you?" He pointed at the faun's crooked, spindley legs and at the cross-eyed dragon's misshapen wings.

"We cannot be touched," said the dragon.

"That's right," said the faun.

"Nonsense," said the penman, and he dipped his quill in the ink again and approached one of the dragon's bent wings. But as he was about to make the elegant stroke that would have corrected the problem, an ominous scratching sound came from the forest.

"The Rasor," said the faun. "It's close by."

A second later, a glinting, sharply pointed beak appeared, and in two strokes had shaved away the trunk of a glorious capital letter P. The P collapsed, monkeys spilling out of its branches, and blue apples rolling around.

"Wicked Rasor!" shouted the monkeys, but they scrambled quickly away, as the Rasor turned toward the penman and his friends, and a scroll rolled out of the Rasor's beak. *I see mistakes here,* it said. *And I'm going to scrape them out.*

It scraped out a piece of the faun's little hoof, which caused the poor creature to limp even more. The Rasor turned toward the dragon.

And you should be disposed of entirely, you cock-eyed idiot.

The penman and the faun jumped on the dragon's back and the scaly, reptilian flier clawed its way along the forest floor, wings once again gamely beating. The Rasor followed, razoring the parchment floor, scraping out tree roots and bushes, and trying to reach the dragon's flapping tail. The penman took out his quill, and filled the air with curlicues and flourishes, which fell around the Rasor.

What are all these loose squiggles doing around here? They must be scraped out immediately.

With the Rasor delayed by the squiggles, the cross-eyed dragon struggled over the forest corridor, the monkeys cheering it along. It ran for miles on its little clawed feet, and finally collapsed. ". . . no good . . . can't go another step . . . all flapped out . . ."

"But you outran the Rasor," said the faun. "It's far behind us now."

". . . let it catch me . . . what's the use . . . you chaps push ahead . . ."

"Come on," said the penman, and he and the faun lifted the dragon and helped it along between them.

"Oh, I'm just a cross-eyed old thing," said the dragon. "I'm going to let the Gumma rub me out."

"Steady," said the penman.

". . . let the Rasor scrape me away . . ."

"It gets like this now and then," said the faun. "I generally play some lighthearted music." The faun took out his pipes of Pan, and played a tune, to which he danced, waving his tail and stumbling around clumsily on his little damaged hooves. He fell over a tree trunk, and tripped on the stones, and it cheered the dragon up enormously.

"He's a marvelous dancer," said the dragon to the penman. "Don't you think?"

"I've never seen anything like it," said the penman.

Nor had he ever seen anything like the falling of dusk in Penman's Paradise. The sky, which had been like bright white paper, grew black in one corner, as if an inkwell had been spilled there, and the inky blackness spread. In very little time it was so black the penman could not see the faun dancing. But then the dragon's eyes began to glow.

"My stage is lit," said the faun, still prancing and stumbling around, his hobbled form caught by the dragon's lamps. He danced, and played his pipes, and a paper moon rose slowly.

The dragon too began to dance, a curious hopping motion. It followed the faun around in a ring, hopping and clucking, beak raised to the moon.

The penman watched the two lame creatures dance, their heads bobbing past him, as they turned in little circles.

"Excellent," he said, as they tripped clumsily past him.

"In the moonlight," said the dragon, "I might be anyone. I might be a chief among dragons, noted for fancy dancing."

"And I," said the faun, "might be Pan himself, with beautiful hooves."

"You are all this and more," said the penman, and joined them in their ring. Holding up his robe with two fingers of each hand, he cavorted with them, his big stomach wobbling, his bald head shining in the paper moonlight. Giving a kick which under normal conditions would have put him in the hospital, he cried, "I'm what I want to be! I'm the pen's transcendency!"

He performed a vigorous pirouette and fell down, belly heaving up like a whale. "Beached," he said. "Beached in the moonlight." He rose up on one elbow, as dragon and faun passed, tails out, heads high. He got to his feet and joined them once more.

They danced until the penman got a stitch in his side and had to sit down again. The dragon and the faun sat down beside him, and they caught their breath, and watched the moon cross the sky. "It is pulled by dragons," said the dragon.

"Then why aren't you among them?" asked the penman.

"They said I'd cause the moon to land in a ditch." The dragon stared upward at the glowing orb, a pained look in its face.

"Never mind," said the faun, "you've very good at other things."

"Yes, being cross-eyed lets me see the tips of both ears at the same time. And that," said the dragon, "is terribly useful."

"Don't pout," said the faun.

"I'm not pouting, I'm watching the moon. It's not going to land in a ditch, and I'm very happy about it."

The penman brought out his pen and inkwell and said, "I'm going to draw you your own moon, and you can carry it across the sky whenever you like." He dipped his pen in the ink and looked at the dragon. "Quarter, half, or full?"

"Full, if you don't mind. I like a big moon."

The penman made that hardest thing of all, a perfect circle, with one unbroken line of his pen. And shining right in front of them was a small, pocketsize moon, which the dragon took tenderly in its claws.

"My own little moon."

"I'll make you a few spares," said the penman, "just in case." And with a few more flourishes, he was able to give the dragon enough moons to last quite awhile.

"One for my tail, one for my head, and I'll put this one between my wings. The dragon looked at its friends. "Do you think I could do a little flying now?"

"Of course," said the penman.

The dragon walked off to get a good start and then came running past, wings flapping. It leapt into the air, wobbled unsteadily at first, and then gradually gained some height, its body lit by the three little moons.

It flew in circles, spiraling higher and higher, and

a soft clucking sound floated down. The penman and the faun watched it flying across the face of the great moon, and then the dragon folded its wings and glided back toward the ground.

"He's losing his balance," said the faun, and raced to where the dragon was descending, moons wobbling. One of them rolled off, and fell straight toward a ditch, but the faun was there to catch it. A moment later, the dragon landed, bouncing a few times and then flapping to a stop.

"You were the envy of the entire sky," said the faun.

"Well, I wouldn't go quite *that* far," said the dragon.

"You were magnificent," said the penman. "You could be seen for miles."

"And I only dropped *one* of the moons."

"And here it is back," said the faun, handing it to his friend. "It's not even wrinkled."

"Perhaps," said the penman, "we should continue on toward the Fair Hand's Labyrinth."

"Let me lead," said the dragon, and with its two eyes shining, and its three moons glowing, it led the way across the remainder of the night.

The big moon disappeared before them, and a little while later, the penman heard a hollow rolling sound from the horizon. "What is that noise?"

"Another page is being turned," said the faun.

The penman watched, as the entire horizon lifted in front of them. Bright sunlight streamed out of it, and the new day dawned.

They walked on, with the sun ahead of them, rising slowly. The exotic birds of Penman's Paradise were singing, and the fabulous flowers were opening.

"I smell vinegar in the air, and gallnuts, and gum," said the penman.

"River ahead!" said the faun. It was a wide flow of ink, cutting swiftly along, the sun rippling off its black, shining surface.

"I'll fly us across," said the dragon. "Climb on."

The penman took out his pen, dipped it in the river of ink, and drew a little boat with a small white sail. "I feel like going boating," he said discreetly. "Wouldn't you all like to go boating too?"

"What a handsome vessel," said the dragon. "Let's give it a fine and distinguished name. Let's call it— *The Cross Eyed Dragon.*"

The penman wrote the name on the bow in rich, flowing letters, and they climbed aboard. The faun pushed off, and they entered the current. The boat started to drift downstream. "We need some wind," said the dragon, and began beating its wings. The sails filled, and the little boat responded, nosing forward across the stream.

"It's a sailor's life for us," sang the dragon, wings flapping.

Inky creatures from the deep broke the surface to look at them, and dove away. Water birds skimmed the surface, and circled the boat, crying cries that made the penman's thoughts dissolve like river foam. He sat in the boat, content to sail forever, until he heard from a still greater distance, from a different world, the meowing of his cat. *She's hungry. I must return.*

"Steady as she goes," said the dragon, its beating wings carrying them to shore.

The faun leapt from the boat and pulled it to land. The penman dipped his quill into the river of ink once more, and with a series of quick, spiraling strokes, wove a fine rope with which to tie the boat.

"All is fast," said the dragon. "She will wait here for the next passengers. She's a good, well-named boat."

They left *The Cross Eyed Dragon* at the shore, and walked on. "When the river is crossed," said the faun, "the Fair Hand's Labyrinth is near."

"Yes," said the dragon, "it could pop out at us anywhere now."

"Does it move around?" asked the penman.

"It seems to move, but who can tell? When we find it, it will be too soon."

They followed the arc of the sun, "for the Labyrinth likes the evening," said the faun, "when the wanderer has grown tired, and things merge and blend in the mind."

The sun of Penman's Paradise traveled, its luminous gold paint shining ever more to the west, and as it dropped down low over the plain of parchment, the Fair Hand's Labyrinth was seen—a maze of extraordinary flourishes, deep and richly inked, as if thousands of decorative scripts had been laid upon each other.

"No one who has entered the Labyrinth has ever come back again," said the faun. "They either find their way out the other side, or they perish within it."

"I know these figures well," said the penman, gazing at the serpentine strokes that formed the Labyrinth.

"They will confound you at every turn," said the faun. "But I see you are determined."

"Somewhere beyond this Fair Hand's Labyrinth my cat is waiting to be fed. Also, my students will be appearing for class, and if I'm not there they will throw ink pots at each other."

"Then we must say goodbye," said the faun.

"I hate goodbyes," said the dragon. "Let's go with him."

"But we're not masters of the pen," said the faun. "We'll get lost in the Fair Hand's Labyrinth and starve."

"Oh, bother," said the dragon, "I don't care." And it put a clawed foot into the Labyrinth, turned once, and was completely disoriented. "I'm lost!"

"Right beside you," said the penman.

So too was the little faun, all three in the first vortex of the Fair Hand's Labyrinth. "Oblique downstrokes and narrow diagonals," said the penman. "Perfectly clear through here." And he led the way through the vortex.

"Don't go too fast!" shrieked the dragon. It sobbed and hung onto the faun.

"Try to stay calm," said the faun.

"I'm cross-eyed. How could I think I'd manage in here?"

". . . four-fold relationship, horizontal to vertical . . ."

"What is he talking about?" whispered the dragon.

"He's finding his way," said the faun.

". . . cross bars two body heights above the tail of the letter f . . ."

"Tails? Why is he talking about tails?" The dragon's tail twitched back and forth.

"It is the secret of proportion," said the little faun.

"It's a terrible strain on a cross-eyed reptile's tiny brain," said the dragon.

They marched on, the penman threading his way carefully through the intricate overlays of penmanship. ". . . grotesque majuscules appearing . . . but they are simple if you relax the hand and eye . . ."

"I have a terrible headache," said the dragon.

". . . derived from the miniscules, don't you see . . ."

"It feels like we're tied up in twine," said the dragon, thrashing its wings. "Strings all over me, knotting and twisting . . ."

"Just look at these marvelous descenders," said the penman, stroking his hand along a group of dangling tails, which hung from huge g's and p's and q's.

"Snakes!" cried the dragon.

"Calm yourself," said the faun, and took the dragon's scaly claw in its hand. "We need only follow the penman."

"Yes, but where is he? All I can see is black spagetti."

"There, just ahead," said the faun.

". . . serifs sweeping upward from the lower parallel . . . nothing difficult here . . ."

"He doesn't think it's difficult," said the dragon, a tear running down its beak.

". . . now here are a number of badly joined letters,

to throw us off the track ..." The penman walked quickly on ahead.

"I'm stepping in worms," sobbed the dragon.

"It's only the little letters of the alphabet," said the faun.

"There's something crawling up my nose."

"It's only the tail of a *p*."

"It feels like a spider."

"Look, the master is waving to us!"

"I can't see anything but spiders!"

"There! He's caught! He can't move!" The faun raced toward the penman's side to help him, but found himself plunging into unutterable confusion; his eyes rolled in his head, a pain struck him between the eyes, and all he could do was sag to the floor of the Fair Hand's Labyrinth.

"Master ... I'm trapped ..."

The penman swayed back and forth dizzily. "My vision ... I'm seeing two of everything ... I can't stand up ..." He too fell down, gaping at a web of designs that made him feel he was in two places at once. He closed his eyes and tried to collect himself, but when he opened them again he didn't know up from down.

"Am I standing or falling? I can't tell."

"... we're dropping, master," cried the faun, "the Labyrinth has claimed us. It is too clever, even for you."

"What's going on?" said the dragon, its voice calm. "Why are you fellows writhing on the ground?" It helped the faun and the penman up.

"You—can see where you're going?"

"Perfectly. It's just a simple corridor you're lying in."

The penman held to one of the dragon's wings and the faun held to the other, and the dragon led them through. "It's the first time I've ever seen well. Very good focus, one of everything, instead of two."

"He's reversed the Labyrinth's plan," said the penman. "Where we see double, he sees single—"

"—because I'm cross-eyed, yes, I suppose that must be it. If all the world were like this, I'd probably be a chief among dragons. Anyway, I wouldn't fly into tree trunks with my head." The dragon walked along briskly, through the cunning corridor which, for the penman and the faun, was impossible to navigate, its double perspectives making them both feel they were walking on their hands.

"You're a most valuable companion," said the penman.

"You've solved the hardest problem of the Labyrinth," said the faun.

"I have, haven't I. Most unusual, being the hero instead of the goat." He caught himself quickly, as he looked at the faun's furry, goat-legs. "Sorry, dear friend, I didn't mean—"

"It's alright, I *am* half-goat, there's no point in denying it."

"Of course, and it's not as if you ate people's laundry."

"I'd never dream of it."

"Exactly," said the dragon. "The goat in you is a gentle sort of beast with awfully good manners."

"What *do* you eat?" asked the penman.

"Oh, the blue apples, and the golden grapes. However," said the faun, "since I'm a mythical creature I could actually live on air."

"Alas," said the penman, "I am unable to." He took out his pen and attempted to draw himself a slice of bread, but each stroke he made was claimed by the Labyrinth—and his slice of bread vanished into the troubling perspectives of the corridor.

"Am I to starve then?"

"I believe—" The dragon reached under its wing and brought out one of its little moons, and gave it to the penman.

It had a lovely aroma of well-cured cheese. "You don't mind?"

"Please," said the dragon. "You're beginning to look pale."

The penman ate the little moon cheese. "Scrumptious."

"Happy you liked it," said the dragon, and then, a moment later, collided with a wall.

"Are you all right?"

"Everything went double again," said the dragon, holding its head.

"We've reached the end of the double corridor," said the penman.

"Can we take a rest?" asked the dragon. "I suddenly feel very tipsy."

The dragon sank down, and the penman and the faun sank down too, for they were exhausted from the difficulties of the Fair Hand's Labyrinth. "They call it Fair," said the dragon. "I should say it's foul. The Foul Hand's Labyrinth."

"Has it always been here?" asked the penman.

"Always."

"And what is its purpose?"

"It's alive," said the faun. "It feeds on those it lures into it."

The dragon groaned. "I feel something nibbling on me." It shrieked and leapt up. "Look, my lines are coming unraveled. Oh my stars! I'm being untied!"

The penman whipped out his quill and ink, and made a quick stroke, rejoining the dragon's lines.

"I too!" cried the faun, looking down in horror, as his hoof lines detached, and began to move away, to be woven into the Labyrinth's design. The penman made another quick stroke to repair the faun, but the unraveling of his friends was proceeding too fast for his quill to follow. He watched in desperation as their dissolution continued.

"Help us, penman! We're dying!"

Half the faun was already gone, woven into the web of strokes that formed a sort of trellis above them. Into it went the dragon's tail, and then its claws and wings.

"Farewell, penman!"

A moment more and the penman stood alone. Dragon and faun had vanished into the intricate mesh that hung overhead.

The penman studied it for a very long time, and discerned, finally, that it was built in cubes. He reached up to the mesh, and traced along it with his finger. "Hmmmmm . . . nine divisions . . . let us call this line *ab*, and this one *cd*. Now then . . . here is the narrow diagonal, and here . . . if I'm not mistaken, is the tip of my dragon's tail."

He pulled and the little bit of tail came out. He continued through the mesh of cubes, until he found the next odd line woven into it, which proved to be another piece of the tail. He joined it to the first, and the two pieces started waving.

He followed along through the cubes. ". . . eighth division, my dragon's spine. Good, come out of there . . ."

He worked, and the dragon started to form again, until it was hopping and dancing about. "I'm back, I'm back! Where was I, penman? Everything was black."

"We must get the faun," said the penman, still working. "Sixth division of the line *ef*—"

"That's his hoof," said the dragon.

"And here's his crooked shin—"

"Yes, yes," said the dragon excitedly, "now comes the knee."

The faun's leg began to prance, and to it the penman added the other leg, then the trunk, the arms, the head, and the little nubby horns.

"Penman!"

"You're whole once again, dear faun."

"Am I really me?" asked the faun. Attempting to skip, he twisted his knee and fell down. Looking up shyly, he said, "I guess I am."

"Certainly you are," said the dragon. "The penman has put us together exactly as we were."

Suddenly, the maze of the Labyrinth grew agitated. All of its cubes were glowing, and its flourishes and curlicues twisted about, snapping and hissing.

"It's angry!"

"We'll all be eaten now!"

The masses of black lines were weaving in and out of themselves, so fast the penman couldn't follow, but the basic design of the maze was changing, was growing more solid, was becoming—

"A door!"

It was ornate, beautiful, with delicate hinges and a finely carved handle.

"We've solved the Fair Hand's Labyrinth," said the penman. "We are free to leave."

"Let us go at once," said the dragon. It grabbed the faun's hand, and stepped toward the door, but owing to its cross-eyes, struck the doorframe instead. Rubbing its beak, it shook its head, bowed to the penman and said, "After you."

"Very well," said the penman. "The other side is freedom, I am sure. But before we enter, because all things are uncertain, let me correct your shapes, now, while I have the power of Penman's Paradise in my hand."

"No," said the dragon.

"But why not? Surely you can't enjoy flying like—like—"

"Like an old flapping boot? That, I admit, is annoying but, you see—"

"—we are what we are," said the faun.

"Poppycock," said the penman.

"I'm just a silly cross-eyed reptile with wings that don't work," said the dragon. "I'm just a mistake, but mistakes are life too. Aren't they?"

"I am a perfectionist. It grieves me to see them."

"Mistakes can be very instructive," said the faun.

The penman lowered his head. The Fair Hand's

Labyrinth had been solved, but his friends, these two living mistakes, were hard to comprehend. He opened the door, the delicate hinges moving smoothly, and waved his friends through. The dragon and the faun stepped out of the Labyrinth and he followed. He was standing on the threshold of his own studio.

"So," he said to himself, "the Fair Hand's Labyrinth leads to the penman's home." He looked quickly around the empty room. "But where is the faun? And where the dragon?"

He opened the doors, called out the windows, looked under the bed. His cat, thinking he was calling her, came and rubbed against his leg. "Dear puss," he said, "they entered just ahead of me, they must be here somewhere." He searched in all the cupboards, sifted through the drawers, even opened up the cookie jar. Exasperated, he slumped down in his chair, and rested his belly against the edge of his desk. And there before him on his drawing board were faun and dragon, fixed and frozen on a piece of clean white parchment.

"My friends, now I can make you whole." He picked up his eraser and lowered it over the dragon's misshapen wings. But something stayed his hand, and he laid the eraser down. He picked up his razor and brought it to the faun's twisted hooves, but again he found himself unable to scrape away the ill-drawn lines. He gazed at the dragon and the faun for a long while, at their flaws and imperfections. Suddenly a cry went through him and he understood: he loved them just as they were.

**   **   **

Penman's Paradise ended with a marvelous flourish of pen strokes. While writing it, my handwriting had been transformed from its usual chicken scrawl into the most beautiful script I'd ever seen. The penman's hand had guided mine.

I turned to a new page in the empty notebook, and as I did so realized a chill had entered the room. I had let the fire die down, so I got up from Uncle's desk and put a few more logs onto the hot coals and stirred them up. Soon I had a great fire blazing in the fireplace, but oddly enough the room remained quite cold. I returned to the desk, and picked up Uncle's pen once more. My cold breath appeared in the air. I was shivering all over. But the faint blue lettering had begun to appear on the page of the empty notebook, and I had to follow it. I heard the sound of whispering blades . . .

Second Tale
From the Empty Notebook

Whispering Blades

The skating rink was old, and had been part of the life of the city for many generations. It stood on the outskirts of town, fed by a stream that came from deep in the forest, and on whose banks a line of cottages stood, cheerful and bright. The rink too was bright, lit by lanterns hanging all along its high wooden fence, which gave the ice a faint glow, and made for lively shadows as the skaters danced, and spun, and raced along. Their sharp skates cut in as they cornered and twirled, the blades etching graceful swirling patterns into the ice. An attendant with a broom swept the ice free of the fine shavings, while another attendant stayed by the door, handing out tickets to the skaters as they entered.

Sabrina had been skating already for several

hours, her hands tucked inside a warm muff, and a fleecy wool cap covering her ears—for the night was crisply cold. She loved to skate, but now her ankles were beginning to ache, and her toes were getting numb, as she skated toward the exit.

"Ticket, please," said the attendant, who had orders not to let anyone out unless they showed their ticket, which was the proof they'd not snuck into the skating rink when no one was looking.

"It's in my muff," said Sabrina, and felt around inside it—but the ticket wasn't there. She took the muff off and shook it, then looked inside it, then held it up to the lantern light in order to peer through it. "I've lost it," she said, and gave the attendant her sweetest smile.

"Then you can't leave," said the attendant, and gave her his meanest frown, for certain children snuck in and out of the rink without paying, and he wouldn't stand for it.

"But I have to get home."

"Then give me your ticket."

"But I told you—I lost it."

"Then buy another one."

"I don't have any money."

"Well, in that case, there's nothing I can do." The attendant planted himself firmly in the exit, blocking Sabrina's way.

She skated off, shocked and close to crying, for no one had ever treated her so rudely before. "I haven't done anything wrong," she said to herself, "I only lost my ticket." And when she skated on past the attendant again, she made her ankles wobble a bit, and lowered her head, and pretended to be shivering. *I'm wretched and miserable,* she said to herself, but the attendant only smiled, and said, "No ticket, no exit."

"But I'm just a little girl!"

"And I'm just a ticket taker. No ticket, no exit."

"Why are you being so mean to me?"

"Because you snuck in here without paying."

"I didn't."

"Then show me your ticket."

Sabrina skated off once more, and now her ankles really did wobble, for she'd been skating already for a very long time.

"You'll be skating all night long," said the attendant, when she came by again.

"My father will have you punished for this," said Sabrina.

"No, he won't. You broke the law."

"No, I didn't."

"Then show me your ticket."

"Oh," sputtered Sabrina, "you're such a stubborn person."

"I'm just the ticket taker."

Sabrina skated off, her ankles bent in, and her head drooping. She circled the rink, but when she passed the ticket taker again she made no attempt to get his sympathy. "I'm not going to whimper or beg that awful person for anything."

Other skaters passed her, and new skaters came onto the ice. She watched enviously as some skaters departed, handing over their ticket at the exit. Soon they'd be home by the fire, and drinking hot drinks. "While I have to keep skating."

"That's right," said the ticket taker, overhearing her conversation with herself, and calling to her. "You'll have to skate all night long."

"I hate you!"

"Why? I'm just the ticket taker."

Sabrina skated on, and on, circling the rink many times, past the hanging lanterns and past the gate. Her muff hung down, and her skates were dragging, but she couldn't stop skating, because then she'd be too cold. Her skates kept skimming over the ice, the blades whispering beneath her. She grew weary, and numb, and still she skated on, and the more tired she got, the louder grew the voice of the whispering blades. After awhile, she could hear nothing else, and with her head drooping down, all she could see was the ice below her. And it was undergoing a remarkable transformation, its opaque white face becoming transparent, like a window.

Through this window at her feet, she saw a world—the world inside the ice. Seeing it, seeing streets and houses and people down there below her skates, she lost her balance, teetered, and fell.

The ice received her, down into itself, Sabrina sinking into a faint bluish translucency. She bounced, on an icy street, in an icy land, with everything around her made of ice.

"Chilly, isn't it," said a cheerful voice beside her.

She looked up and saw a man whose body was made of ice. His smiling mouth revealed a row of teeth like ice-cubes, and his cheeks were sparkling with frost.

"Yes," answered Sabrina, as she stared at him, "it certainly is chilly."

"And a very good thing too," said the man of ice. He slapped his hands together and crystals of ice flew into the air. "It can't get cold enough for me."

"Well, it's already too cold for *me*," said Sabrina, as she huddled her hands inside her muff and rubbed it up and down on her stomach. She looked at the icy facade of the buildings, and the icy sidewalks. The man of ice leaned over her, and said, not unkindly, "Lost your ticket, I suppose."

"Yes!" cried Sabrina excitedly. "Do you have one you can give me?"

"I'm not connected to the establishment."

"Oh, what a shame."

"But would you care for some sweet ices?"

"There's already too much ice."

"Ah, but sweet ice is different." The man of ice removed an ice-blue cup from his belt, and banged it into a snow bush. Crystals of ice fell off and filled the cup and then he led Sabrina over to a large crystalline tree in the center of the city square. It had a spigot on it, just like a public fountain. "Syrup, you know," he said, and turned on the spigot. The syrup ran over the ice chips, and did look quite delicious.

"I see you don't have a cup either," said the man of ice, as he withdrew his cup from the spigot.

"I have a muff," said Sabrina.

"Yes, but you can't eat sweet ices from a muff." He sighed, and gave her his own cup. She put it to her lips, and though it was cold, it was very good, and she felt better at once for having drunk it. She

handed the cup back to the man of ice and said, "Thank you very much. But now I simply must be going."

"Do you always use people's cups and then leave them the moment you've finished?"

"I didn't mean to be rude. But I'm standing here on my ice skates and my ankles are getting tired."

"Snow ponies."

"Snow ponies?"

"Yes, we'll hail one."

The man of ice held up his hand as first one snow pony and then another came by, pulling little snow-sleighs, but the ponies just kept right on going, up the block.

"Of course, they're temperamental. Some of them won't stop."

"But why not?" whined Sabrina.

"Well, it's entirely up to a snow pony if it wants to stop. Isn't it? I mean, that should be obvious, shouldn't it?"

"Let me try," said Sabrina.

"Why? Do you know something about snow ponies I don't?"

"I think," said Sabrina, holding up her muff, "it's just a matter of good manners." She waved her muff in a polite way, with delicacy and tact, and a snow pony stopped. Its sled was made of rather dirty ice, and the pony itself was shabby in appearance, with a dirty mane, and a tail full of knots.

"Tell it how beautiful it is," whispered the man of ice.

Sabrina stroked the snow pony's mane. "I've never

seen such a pretty, sparkling mane. It's as bright as the stars."

The snow pony nuzzled her muff, and then turned its head toward its cart, as if asking her to step into it, which she did, along with the man of ice. The moment they were settled the pony started to trot.

"Where are we off to?" asked Sabrina.

"That's up to the snow pony," said the man of ice.

"Well," said Sabrina, "it would be much nicer if we had a blanket to wrap around us."

"Surely you're joking."

"A lovely warm blanket would be oh so nice."

"A lovely warm blanket would be *ghastly*," said the man of ice. "I can't think how you can be so thoughtless as to suggest it."

"Because I'm cold."

"Cold is the perfect condition. Cold hands, cold feet, cold nose. If you've got those, you should feel lucky indeed."

"I've got them and I feel terrible."

"Then you're a very mixed-up little girl."

I'm not mixed-up, said Sabrina to herself. I'm cold. But I see it's no use telling this person about it.

"Ice water in the veins," said the man of ice, with a gesture of well-being. "And a cold heart. That's the standard."

He'll never understand, thought Sabrina to herself.

"Cold soup, cold socks, cold coffee. Cold towels, cold bath, cold pajamas."

He's probably unmovable on this particular subject, she reflected to herself, and huddled her arms to the elbows inside her muff.

"Did I mention cold fish? Mustn't forget cold fish."

Sabrina rubbed her hands together and stamped her feet inside her skates, while the man of ice continued to hold forth on the subject of things cold.

"There's nothing I like more than to sit down in an ice-cold chair in the evening and put my feet up on a block of ice, and read the icepapers. Sounds wonderful, doesn't it?"

"Yes, delightful."

"And then, when I'm tired, I climb into my freezing cold bed and cover myself with snow. There's nothing like a good, frosty night's sleep to refresh both mind and body. Then when I wake up in the morning, I take a—"

"—cold shower."

"That's right! What a pleasant little girl you are. And so bright too. I must help you in whatever way I can."

The snow pony had been trotting along at a brisk pace, but now it began to slow, and a moment later it stopped completely, in front of a large, old rooming house, made of ice.

"I think," said the man of ice, "this is as far as the silly beast is going."

"But where are we?"

"I'm sure I don't know. But one thing I do know, and that is that there's nothing more stubborn than a snow pony. And it means to stand here until we climb off." They climbed off, and the pony gazed at them, its blue, translucent eyes filled with its own ideas about things. "Well," said the man of ice, "we might as well see what's what with this house."

Sabrina followed him, for her situation couldn't get any worse, she felt, and just possibly things might improve in unexpected ways. So she waited, very properly, as the man of ice knocked on the door. A landlady, made of ice, answered it, and looked past them, to the curb. "It's that pony again," she said, and then looked back at them. "Well, you might as well come in."

They followed her into the dining room, where the boarders of the rooming house were seated around the table. There were four of them, all gruff and sour looking. There was also a snow white cat, sleeping in a basket. The basket, the drapes, and all the furniture were of ice.

"Sit down," said the elderly woman, and pointed to a pair of empty chairs. Sabrina sat down, beside one of the sour-looking boarders. "Does the pony often come here?" she asked the landlady.

"Yes, I don't know why."

"How strange."

"You certainly chatter a lot," said the sourpuss beside Sabrina, and she looked at him, her feelings hurt. But he didn't seem to notice, he was spooning up his soup.

"My soup has gotten warm." He looked at the landlady. "How did that happen?"

"Yes, mine is warm too," said one of the other boarders, his face just as sour.

"And mine," said the third.

"And what is more," said the fourth, "there's no ice in my glass."

"Who are these people?" Sabrina asked the man of ice in a whisper.

"Oh, they're just a bunch of grumps," said the man of ice.

"What're you whispering about?" grumbled one of the grumps.

"Nothing," said Sabrina. "I was just wondering where the fireplace is."

"The fireplace!"

"Help!"

"Good heavens!"

"Really, how disgusting!"

Everyone yelled at her, and Sabrina cowered behind her muff. "I just thought the cat might like it."

"The cat wouldn't like it."

Sabrina leaned back toward the man of ice. "These people don't seem to have a very good disposition."

"Yes, well, you see—they're grumps."

One of the grumps stood up, and pointed his fork. "I heard that. And perhaps we are a bit grumpy when our cold soup gets warm, and when people ask where the fireplace is. But the important question, the real question that must be asked is—who is this impertinent little girl?"

"She lost her ticket," said the man of ice. "And she can't get out."

"A likely story," said the grump.

"It's true," said Sabrina, her lower lip turning downward.

"She's pouting," said one of the other grumps. "How I *hate* little girls who pout."

"Then why don't you act a little nicer?" asked the man of ice.

"Who are you?"

"An interested party."

"A busybody," said the third grump. "That's what you are, a busybody. You burst in when people are having their cold soup, and then it gets warm."

The landlady banged her shoe on the table. "Will you all please shut up."

"I'm sorry," said Sabrina softly.

"Yes," said the man of ice, "we didn't mean to disturb you."

"It's that pony," said the landlady. "It always brings strangers around at suppertime."

"Perhaps we should go," said Sabrina.

"Go?" sniffed one of the grumps. "Where could you possibly go? You've lost your ticket, haven't you?"

"Yes."

"Then you might as well stay right where you are."

"Why?"

"Because," said the grump, "I have a ticket upstairs."

"And you'll give it to me?"

"Yes. If you promise not to thank me. Or undergo any other emotional displays. I don't like warmth in a person, I must tell you."

"Very well," said Sabrina, "I'll be cold as ice."

"That remains to be seen," said the grump. He stood up from his chair and walked to the staircase outside the dining room. "This way."

Sabrina followed him to the steps, clumping along on her skates. The grump looked down at her skates, his forehead creased with a grumpy frown. "Don't you ever take those off?"

"I haven't anything else to wear, and my feet will get cold if I take them off."

"Harumpf," said the grump, and proceeded up the stairs, with Sabrina following, her hands tightly gripping the icy stair railing as she stumbled up on her skates.

"This way," grumbled the grump impatiently, as he waited for her in the hall. He opened a frozen door, and she followed him into a frozen room. There was a frozen bed, and a small frozen trunk. The grump sat on the bed, looked at Sabrina, shook his head peevishly, and then opened the trunk. "I know it's in here ... somewhere," he said, rummaging around in the trunk.

"I hope you find it."

The grump looked up at her. "Would you mind not interrupting me?"

"Sorry."

"... overly talkative little girl ... bossing people around ..."

"I only said I hope you find it."

"Must you repeat it too?"

"You certainly are grumpy."

"I'm a grump. How else is a grump supposed to act? A grump is supposed to act grumpy and that's all there is to it. No room for change. But there are a great many ways for little girls to act, and I suggest you choose one that isn't so offensive."

A tear trickled down Sabrina's face. The grump

looked up from under his frosty eyebrows. "No! Don't cry! You'll melt my rug."

Sabrina quickly wiped away the tear. "I can't do anything right," she sobbed, adding an extra little bit of pathetic choking.

"Yes, you can, you can stop boo-hooing in my room." The grump knocked things about in his trunk, and then suddenly shouted, "Ah ha!" He raised his hand triumphantly, and held it out toward Sabrina. Clutched in his fingertips was a worn and faded but definitely authentic ticket.

"I told you it was here. Take it."

He thrust it at her and she took it, quickly, before he changed his mind.

"You have exquisite manners, little girl," he said testily. "You might have cracked my fingers off."

"I was just so eager—"

"Yes, I'm sure you had *every* reason."

Sabrina stared in wonder at the ticket. "Where did you get this?"

"I was once a warm, cozy being like you. I much prefer being a cold-hearted, uncomfortable grump, of course, but that doesn't change the fact that I used to be a little boy. And when I was a little boy I went skating one night, and I lost my ticket. I wound up here in the Land of Ice and by the time I found my ticket, I'd turned into an ice person, and here I have remained. Happily, I might add. Happy to be a grump. De-*lighted* to indulge in all the grumpiness I want. Little girl, are you listening to me?"

"I was listening," said Sabrina, "but I suddenly got very worried that I'm turning into an ice person."

She looked down nervously at her feet to see if they were turning into ice.

"But you have a ticket now."

"Yes, that's right. Oh, thank you!" Sabrina leapt toward the grump, arms extended.

He leapt back, horrified. "No affection, *please*. I can't stand it, especially from sweet little girls."

Sabrina put her ticket in her muff. "How soon does it take for a person, a small person, to turn to ice?"

"It sneaks up on you."

"I wonder if it's sneaking up on me right now."

"Probably."

"Then what am I to do? Skate as fast as I can?"

"Not the answer."

"Well, what is the answer?"

"If I knew the answer, I wouldn't be made of ice today."

"Did all the boarders in this house lose their tickets?"

"It's not something we discuss."

Sabrina hurried out of the room, skated down the frozen hall, and stomped on down the stairs, into the parlor. "The man who accompanied you here is gone," said the landlady. "He said to tell you he was sorry, but he had to go back to town."

Sabrina's hopes sagged. The grump who'd given her the ticket pushed past her into the parlor, to join the other grumps, who were standing around a piano, singing chilly songs.

"Won't you please help me?" she cried, and acted as absolutely pathetic as she could, but the grumps were busy harmonizing, out-of-tune.

The pony, thought Sabrina, I must find the pony. But then she remembered that the pony would only bring her back to this house, because that's where it always brought people.

The grumps are my only hope, she said to herself, and I must make them pay attention to me.

"Does anyone have any hot cocoa?"

"Hot cocoa?" snapped one of the grumps. "How dare you."

"Hot, she said hot."

"Hot, hot, hot!" shrieked Sabrina. "Hot baths, hot water bottles, and hot soup! Heat waves! Burning pavement!"

"Stop!" growled a grump.

"I feel faint," said another.

"My ears are burning," said the third.

"I've never heard such terrible language," said the grump who'd given her the ticket. "Is this the thanks I get?"

"You said you didn't want any thanks," pouted Sabrina. "And what good is a ticket if I don't know where to take it?"

"I suppose," said the first grump, "she'd like us all to drink hot cocoa and melt into the floor."

"Call the police, that's all," said the second grump.

"If you won't help me," said Sabrina, "I don't know what I'll do." She sobbed bitterly, and stumbled around the room, clinging to the ice furniture to keep from falling; her wool cap tipped into her eyes, her ankles twisted, and her muff dropped on the floor.

"Oh very well," grumbled the others.

"Because if we don't help her, she'll just go on being pathetic."

"And if we *do* help her, we just might get rid of her."

"Precisely why I gave her the ticket."

Sabrina looked at the grumps, and wondered how they could be so mean.

"Don't look at us like that."

"We *are* grumps, you know."

"Grouchy, gloomy, and grim."

"And we don't like little girls."

"I thought," said Sabrina softly, "maybe you did like me, just a little."

"Well, we don't."

The grumps put on their ice coats and ice boots and ice hats, grumbling all the while they did so. But finally they were ready, and followed her outside into the street.

"How did you get here in the first place?" they asked her.

"I skated around and around until I grew very tired, and then suddenly I was here."

"Well, if you try skating backwards, around and around until you grow very tired, maybe suddenly you *won't* be here."

"And wouldn't that be wonderful."

"But," said Sabrina, "I don't know how to skate backwards."

"Why not?"

"Because it takes lots of practice."

"Of all the silly reasons—"

"I knew she'd be difficult."

"I suppose we'll just have to show her how."

Though they weren't wearing skates, the grumps demonstrated how one skates backwards. They looked quite stuffy as they did so, hands clasped behind their backs, noses in the air, but Sabrina had to admit that they had a certain grumpy grace.

"All right, you try."

Sabrina tried. She bumped into grumps, and the grumps fell down.

"I knew it!"

"She did that deliberately."

"—the worst sort of little girl."

"Get anywhere near one of them and you're in trouble."

"Please," said Sabrina, "I'm sorry. Can't we try again?"

"Hang onto our hands. And don't try any funny business." The grumps pushed her gently backwards, and though there was a great deal of grumbling, they finally managed to give her the feel of the thing—and suddenly she was freely skating backwards, very beautifully, all upon her own.

She skated backwards up the street, and the grumps had to hurry along to keep up with her. She turned at the corner and skated backwards around the block, several times, with the grumps cheering her on each time she went by. But though she skated until she was tired, though she looked down wearily at the icy street where her skates were gliding, she did not sink through, or undergo any sort of transformation toward home.

"But," she said, as she skated up to the grumps again, "I feel much warmer."

They jumped away from her.

"Perhaps not warm," she added quickly. "But less icy."

"You take her skating and what does she do?"

"Uses bad language."

"Don't you know—*ice is nice?*"

They peered at her, scowls written across their faces. She'd never seen them look so grumpy, and she suspected it was because they hadn't been able to get rid of her. "Ice *is* nice," she said. "I didn't mean to suggest it wasn't."

"Harumpf."

The grumps grumbled and grumped, and trudged along the street, as Sabrina skated beside them. ". . . have to get her out of our hair."

"One of those impossible little girls you always fear will show up."

". . . must think of something."

"Well, I *gave* her a ticket."

"Yes, you fool, but it wasn't enough."

Oh dear, thought Sabrina, if they don't stop grumping, they'll *never* think of something.

"Grumps," she said, "could you please just concentrate."

"Did you hear that? Has there ever been such a bossy child?"

"She's an exasperating little beast."

"—makes me want to scream."

"—or do something rash." Saying so, the grump who'd given Sabrina a ticket threw open his ice-coat, removed it, and jumped up and down on it. "There," he said, "that's how grumpy *I* feel."

Sabrina stared at him in wonder, for she certainly never thought she could be the cause of so much discomfort in a person, even an ice person, that they would rip off their coat and jump up and down on it.

"I'm terribly sorry if I upset you."

"Please don't make matters worse by apologizing."

"Do you know," said Sabrina, "that your chest is transparent?"

"It's rude to stare."

"Yes, and inside of it I see a skating rink! In the moonlight! For a heart you have a skating rink, just like mine back home."

"I assure you, my heart is a solid ball of ice, with icicles dripping off it."

"No, it's not, it's a skating rink in the moonlight. Look at it glowing."

The other grumps gathered around. "She's right, old boy. Your heart is a skating rink."

The grump looked down over the end of his nose toward the glow in his chest. "Well, if it is, she's the cause of it."

"It's beautiful," said Sabrina.

"But entirely abnormal," said one of the other grumps, removing his coat. "Now, as you can see, my chest is opaque. Frozen solid. And the heart beneath it is the regulation ball of ice."

"No, it's not."

"It's not?" The grump looked down, and to his amazement saw the glow of a skating rink in his own chest. "It must be contagious," he said with alarm.

The other two grumps quickly removed their coats.

"Good heavens!"

"We've all got skating rinks in our chests!"

They looked at Sabrina.

"It's her fault, of course."

"I believe it's starting to itch."

"Yes, well, it's because of all those little skaters in there."

"It feels terribly congested."

Sabrina lifted the edge of her wool cap off her ears, for as the tiny skaters went around inside the grumps, their little skates made a soft whispering sound, and it whispered to her. "Grumps," said Sabrina, "join hands in a ring."

"Listen to her. We're in agony and she wants to play."

"You're *not* in agony," said Sabrina. "It's a perfectly lovely skating rink. Now join hands. That's it. And circle around me."

"What a tiresome child."

"Can you imagine what she'll be in a few years?"

"—skaters going around inside us—"

"Very well, we've joined hands."

"Now," said Sabrina, "dance around me in a ring."

"What a perfectly horrible idea."

"Dance around you? I'd rather sit on a hot stove."

"Don't talk back," said Sabrina brusquely. "Just do as I say."

"I can't believe this child is ordering us around."

"Dance," commanded Sabrina. "Dance like the very nice grumps you are."

"We're *not* nice."

"We're not *supposed* to be nice."

"But if we do a little two-step, we might get rid of her."

"Anything, anything," said the fourth grump. "Let's just get it over with."

The grumps danced around Sabrina, performing a little two-step, hands held together, toes out, then in.

"Shuffle, and—once again—"

"I suppose she wants us to sing too."

"If you would, please."

"Oh, anything your Royal Snootiness wishes, of course."

The four grumps sang, out-of-tune. And as they sang, and danced in a ring, the little skaters within their chests all joined their hands and skated in rings—four rings glowing in the light of four tiny moons.

Sabrina turned as the grumps danced past her, her eyes going from grump to grump, and to the rings of skaters within them. The grumps danced faster, and so did the skaters, and Sabrina turned dizzily, round and round, and then fell down, to the sound of tiny whispering blades.

"I'm back!"

The city of ice was gone. She was seated on the ice of the skating rink back home, on which the moonlight shone. The grumps were gone too; in their place four young boys were skating around her, round and round.

But their caps and cloaks were from a bygone time, as were their skates and gloves. Sabrina stared at them, afraid to speak, for the boys seemed in a frag-

ile state, as their skating slowed, and they looked around the rink.

"How different it is," said one of them.

"Yes," said another, pointing toward the shadowy cottages that stood beyond the rink. "There were no cottages there, only trees."

"And those lanterns, I don't remember them," said the third boy.

"And this girl," said the fourth boy, "look how peculiarly she's dressed. I've never seen clothes like hers before."

Well, thought Sabrina, I've never seen clothes like yours either. But she said nothing, for she'd already caused quite enough trouble with her comments on things.

"We must get out of here," said one of the boys.

"Do you have tickets?" asked Sabrina.

"No. And we've been skating here for such a long time."

They're my grumps, thought Sabrina to herself. But how can I tell them that? She fingered the battered old ticket within her muff, and gazed at each of their faces, but she couldn't tell which of these red-cheeked boys was the grump who'd befriended her and given her the ticket from his frozen trunk. But she knew she couldn't leave him, or the others, behind.

"We mustn't stay on this ice any longer," she said. "We'll have to escape."

"Yes!" shouted the boys. They skated with her, slowly around the rink. The ticket taker's huge form still blocked the exit, and escape would not be possible there. They skated on by him, and circled to the back of the rink, where it was more dimly lit.

"I'm getting so weary," said one of the boys. "It feels like I've been skating forever."

"Don't sink down," chided Sabrina with alarm. "You must stay awake."

"The blades of my skates," said the boy, "are whispering to me."

Sabrina grabbed him by the arm, and spun him roughly about. "Stay awake!" she cried, and shoved him, as hard as she could. He flew backwards, striking the fence. There was a creaking sound behind him, and the board he'd struck pivoted loose.

"Through here," he said, at once wide awake, and led the way, out behind the loose board, while the other boys hid his form with their large, old cloaks.

"Go on," they said to Sabrina, "now you go." She crept through, and the other boys followed her, out into the soft snow beyond the rink.

"I recognize none of it," said one of them, "except the stream." And he pointed to the moonlit surface of the snaking stream that fed the rink. "How long have we been gone?" asked another of the boys, scratching underneath the ancient pattern of his cap.

"Just a few hours," said the third boy. But Sabrina saw a fearful look coming into his eyes.

"Do you live nearby?" she asked.

"Just up the stream," they answered. "And we'd best be going now."

She followed them, onto the ice that covered the stream, and she and the four boys skated up it, toward the cottages on its shores. But when the first boy knocked upon the door of his cottage he wasn't recognized. Nor did his family live there anymore.

He staggered back toward the stream, his face stricken white in the moonlight. "They're gone," he said. "They left fifty years ago."

It was the same at the other cottages. The boys were not recognized, and their families had long ago moved away.

"Come with me," said Sabrina, and she led the four boys up the stream to her own cottage. They crossed through the frozen snow of the yard, their skates crunching on the crust. "When the light from inside falls upon you," she said, "you will have a home."

The door opened, and the light streamed out, onto Sabrina, and the four skaters in their ancient, beautiful cloaks. "Well," said Sabrina's father, "what have we here?"

◦◦◦   ◦◦◦   ◦◦◦

The warmth came back to my fingers, and Uncle's study was once more a cozy place. But how cold it had seemed! I walked to the fireplace and stretched my hands out to the fire. The clock on the wall began to chime. It was two in the morning. My eyes were tired, and my wrist was sore from all the furious scribbling I'd been doing in the empty notebook. But I knew I wasn't finished yet—a wisp of smoke from the fireplace twisted up toward me, and curled itself around my hand, as if to lead me back to the desk. Obeying, I sat down once again, and turned to a new page of the empty notebook. The faint blue lettering appeared once more, and waited for me to trace it. I lifted my pen toward the inkwell. It was filled with mist, like a genie in a bottle. I dipped my nib into the mist, and began to write . . .

Third Tale

From the Empty Notebook

T

Diligence

Lucas held the reins lightly as he moved his carriage through the fog. "No one stirrin'," said the grizzled cabman to himself, and the carriage wheels creaked, the lantern swung gently back and forth, and his head kept falling forward, chin burying itself onto his chest. The mist swirled about his face and covered his horses' flanks with a fine web of moisture. Doorways of buildings appeared for a moment, and then were lost as the mist rolled over them again. "The sort of night that ghosts go walkin'," he said and, as if to answer him, a wavering light appeared in the mist, bobbing back and forth like a disembodied head of supernatural incandescence.

The mist parted round the floating head, to reveal one of the city's lamplighters, whose torch, held aloft, had been the apparition in the fog. The lamplighter called up to the driver. "Any business?"

"A rat asked for a ride to his hole, but that's all," said Lucas. "I'd be better off at home, for I recently boiled a pot of soup. Climb on, we'll go have some."

"I've had your soup before," said the lamplighter. "I found a rusty nut at the bottom of my bowl, along with a piece of your bridle." He took a step back into the mist, his torch held aloft. "I've many wicks to fire." With another step backward, his form vanished completely, only his torch remaining, becoming a bobbing head once again, then fading slowly, then gone.

Lucas flicked his reins. "Just the mention of that lovely soup has filled me with the need for it." He reined his horses toward home, for he was seeing a glowing fire, and his old stuffed chair beside it. "And puss'll be on my lap, and I'll settle a number of important state affairs, and make a pronouncement or two, and pretty soon I'll be asleep, dreamin' I'm king of the moon."

"I say there! Carriage man!"

Lucas's head snapped back up, and he saw a gentleman, half covered by fog, standing near the curb with his hand in the air.

"Yes sir, where to?" Lucas leaned down and opened the door of the carriage, and as he did so, saw that the gentleman was accompanied by another. "That feller don't look too healthy," said Lucas, for the figure was ghostly pale, a wisp of a man, his face as gray as his cloak. And as he stepped into the cab, it

seemed to Lucas he wasn't there at all, that it was just a swirl of mist he had for a passenger.

The horses, sensing something unnatural, bolted. The carriage door swung closed with a bang, and the gentleman on the street had to leap upon the backboard, where he steadied himself, clinging to the carrying rungs.

Lucas stood up and hauled on the reins. "Ho, there! Ho, you blackguards!" But the horses had been seized by passion, and the street echoed with the clatter of their racing hoofbeats. Lucas fought the reins, while the man on back held on for life—and yet a faint smile crossed his lips.

Lucas was thrown backward on his seat, hitting down with a thump. "Whoa, you worthless donkeys! Whoa, I say!" He stood up again, wrapping the reins over his shoulders and hauling with all the strength he had.

The lantern rattled, banging back and forth beside the man on back. "Let them run!" he called to Lucas.

"They'll kill us, sir!"

"Then killed we'll be!"

Warehouses and loading platforms flew past on either side of the racing carriage, but Lucas had only a vague notion of where he was, for all his concentration was on holding back the plunging horses. "No good," he muttered to himself, "it's cut free or die—" He leaned forward to sever the horses from their traces but before his knife was out of its sheath he saw the end of the pier up ahead, the black water waiting to claim horses, carriage, and riders. "Jump, sir, jump for your life!"

The horses' hooves were already beating thin air, as the carriage bumped off the end of the pier. Wheels spinning, it fell toward the water, parting the mist like a ship that has just been launched.

"Blast you, blast!" cried Lucas, cracking his whip with fury and hauling the heads of his horses upward. They leapt desperately, as their hooves touched water.

"Up, up, you rogues! Show me what you're made of!" Lucas's whip cracked like a cannon, and the horses beat their hooves wildly. Their neck muscles quivered, their great haunches bulged with the strain, and Lucas's soul lifted with them. The carriage floated in the air, with the water lapping at its spinning wheels, trying to claim the carriage for its own murky depths. The wheels spun, then slowed, and then hung still, as the carriage rose in the air. The horses whinnied, tossed their heads triumphantly, and the water was left below.

The man on back looked down, adjusted his top hat, and called to Lucas. "What sort of carriage is this, my good fellow?"

" 'Tis a make they call Diligence, sir, but I never expected this from her." Lucas looked around him, at the mist hissing past his floating carriage, and at the swaying backs of his horses, who were climbing still higher on the wind. "We've defied the lawr of somethin' nor other." Lucas tried to see down through the fog, and shook his head. "And there's probably a fine for it, but—" He turned to the man on back, and smiled. "—they'll have to catch us first now, won't they?"

At this, a gray face peered from the carriage window. Lucas looked toward it, startled to remember that another traveled with them. He opened the panel behind him and called down into the carriage. "Is all well in there?" There was no response.

"He don't say much, does he?" Lucas looked at the man on back. "I mean, considerin' we're flyin' through the air."

The carriage suddenly broke through the mist, rising above it, as onto a moonlit plain.

"Great Caesar's ghost!" cried Lucas, "I never seen such beauty."

The moonlit plain of clouds stretched out to the horizon, softly rolling, gently changing, the white magic of the night sky. Below all had been churning fog, but here above the mist it was serene, the moon bathing the tops of the clouds in radiance as far as the eye could see—a fleecy field borne in the darkness.

The man on back leaned toward the window of the coach, and tapped lightly on the glass. "Our horses found the moonlight path."

The gray figure within seemed to nod, then sank back into shadow.

The horses galloped on, and their bridle bells made an icy tinkling sound, and there was indeed a path—a band of light that hung down from the moon itself. "We've struck good road," said Lucas, the reins still dangling in his hands, but it was the horses now who led the way, as if in their long nights of clopping through the city they'd foreseen this pathway through the clouds.

"What magic have we fallen into?" asked Lucas of the man on back, who shook his head. "Our course has been influenced by the one inside." He nodded toward the carriage door.

"And who may that be? I'm not one to pry into matters that go on inside my coach, but seeing as we're out here like bats, I think perhaps I should know."

"I met him outside Casino Mundo, where I'd gone to play a few hands." The man on back ran two white-gloved fingers along the smooth brim of his hat. "My name is Erlwine. I have some skill with cards."

"Well, fancy," said Lucas, "so do I." On his only visit to Casino Mundo, he'd lost the very clothes off his back, and had to go home wrapped in his horse's blanket and nosebag. "And was our passenger—" He nodded toward the door. "—in there too?"

"He was outside the casino, as if waiting for someone, but his manner was confused." Erlwine tapped the top of his hat, fastening it securely against the wind through which they climbed. "I believe I alone saw him. He's not human, you see."

"Not human? Well, what is he then?"

"He's made of fog and light."

Lucas looked down at the carriage window, from which a faint glow came. "I'm used to rain, and fog, and snow. I've carried thieves, and who knows, perhaps a murderer or two, for all things come a coachman's way."

He gazed up at the crystalline rings of stars, and the enormous face of the moon, and then back down at the shrouded earth, where his stuffed chair

waited, and his pot of soup, and his cat, who'd be wondering where her supper was.

"He is a creature of the dark," said Erlwine. "And yet he'd lost his way somehow."

"Perhaps he suffered a blow. I was banged over the head with an ale mug once, and it caused me consid'rable confusion."

"He could have come from the lamppost's glow, or from the eyes of a lynx. But he's slipped out of his proper dimension and we, apparently—" Erlwine gestured with his white-gloved hand up the moon's white path. "—are taking him back."

Lucas gazed down at the frothing, floating stuff on which they traveled. "Like cream of potato soup with an egg yolk whipped into it." He reached over and scooped some up with his hat, then dipped his finger into the mixture and tasted it. "Paprika too." He smacked his lips and drank the contents of his hat. "They make a nice soup, whoever they are."

Erlwine reached down, and scooped some in his hand. "This is silk, my man, with pure gold thread sewn in it." The gambler drew a length of it between his hands. "Look how fine the fibers are."

"You take silk, I'll take soup," said Lucas, and helped himself to another hatful, while Erlwine wound lengths of the beautiful fiber in his hands, for each of us receives from the moonlight what we imagine it to be, and the Diligence climbed on, its lantern swaying and rattling.

"Good gravy, Erlwine, look what's above us!" Lucas pointed with his whip to a castle, fleece-like and white, toward which the path was heading. The horses saw it, and tossed their manes and bridles in excitement.

"Steady on," said Erlwine from the backboard, and his gambler's eyes narrowed, studying the moat which was lowering in the face of the castle. It was misty, golden, insubstantial, and yet it held together as the horses raced across it and into the courtyard of clouds.

Immediately, guards in cloud armor gathered around, holding bows of fog strung with threads of moonlight. But their hands were unable to release the latch on the door of this carriage from the earth, their wispy fingers passing through it. Lucas reached down with his whip and tripped the latch, and Erlwine leapt from the back of the carriage and came round to open the door.

The passenger stepped down, and Lucas saw him more clearly now—for the passenger had gained vitality up here in his own element. He was a young person of regal bearing, and his face was no longer gray, but lit by tones of yellow light, his hair especially, a crown of curls as golden as the harvest moon. His cloak now had a satiny sheen, his shirt front was creamy white, and his evening suit was black cloth spun from spells of darkness. His eyes were bright, but gentle, like pools of water in which the moon was reflected, and he was unmistakably the royal heir of this cloudy region. He turned to Erlwine and Lucas. Mist poured from his lips and Lucas heard a strange language, like tones of music, like raindrops on glass, like thin silver chimes.

"He means for us to follow," said Erlwine, and he

and Lucas moved along with the cloud guard across the courtyard, Lucas eyeing the cloudy cobblestones suspiciously, but they supported him. "Magic, of course," said Erlwine. The gambler felt he'd passed this way before, but when? And where? He seemed to recognize the liquid tones of the host's words, a voice he'd heard while playing cards, a voice which more than once had told him how to play his hand.

They entered beneath a lancet archway, into the castle. Above them was a vaulted ceiling and upon the walls burned torches fed by pitch that seemed to be the night itself. "I'm uneasy," said Lucas softly to Erlwine. "We're sailin' up here like balloons."

Their host led them into a chamber, where he took the central seat, guards on either side of him. Then his cloud ministers came, and a court magician, ancient, bent, cloaked in a dark shroud. This entity, it seemed, had caused the carriage to be lifted, was keeping it afloat now, along with horse, Erlwine, and Lucas—or so said the voice that now filled Lucas' head. *I am Stilla Galbanum, sorceror to his majesty, Prince Nimbus.* The sorceror bowed toward the young prince seated in the central chair. *His majesty thanks you for your assistance.*

I know this place, thought Lucas. It comes and goes above the waterfront, don't it, it comes and goes.

You are here by enchantment, but not for long. The sorceror turned toward Prince Nimbus. *Your majesty, speak quickly. They will understand you now.*

Nimbus spoke. The soft chiming sound of his words had modulated toward the human range. Lucas and

Erlwine heard a pellucid voice, pure as little metal bells. "I am in love, gentlemen, and I need your help."

Erlwine and Lucas drew closer, but before the prince could say more, Stilla Galbanum groaned and bent over, his bony white hands clawing at the air. "The spell . . . is ended . . ."

The floor beneath Lucas and Erlwine began to open; their feet and legs were sinking through the mist. The prince leapt up, and shot a command to his sorceror, who croaked an incantation and waved a stone-tipped wand, but Lucas and Erlwine were falling. Lucas swam frantically in the mist, and slowed his descent enough to land upright in the courtyard where his carriage was parked. But it too was sinking. He ran toward it, and dove, tumbling onto its roof, with Erlwine behind him.

The moonlit path still shone in the clouds below, and the horses righted themselves and the carriage, spinning it slowly around until its wheels were skimming down along the moonbeam's path. Erlwine clung to the rear, while casting a glance at the road behind them, which was breaking up and floating away into amorphous shapes.

Lucas's whip cracked like thunder in the clouds and his horses raced madly down the moonspun slope, aware that its solidity was a dying spell. The mist swirled around them, and Lucas strained to see the enchanted road, but its glow was feeble now. Lucas smelt the river, an aroma of reed and fish and coal from the stacks of barges. "Head up!" he cried to his snorting horses, their own nostrils filled with fear as they raced toward the waterfront. The moon road vanished and the pier suddenly clattered beneath them.

"Made it!" cried Lucas.

Erlwine released the breath he'd been holding, and rubbed his gloved fingers around his hat brim. "Well done."

"I should say well done." Lucas brought the carriage to a halt between warehouses. "Them are good horses, them are."

The two men looked toward the end of the pier, but the road of moonlight was gone, and the mist shrouded everything. "We should speak of this to no one," said Erlwine.

"Erlwine, do you have that cloth you collected?"

Erlwine searched his pockets in vain.

"Sure," said Lucas, "that's how fairy gifts always turn out. A handful of nothing. But what did he want down here, Erlwine? Who was he after?"

Erlwine was unable to answer, not then, nor during succeeding nights upon the waterfront when he worked his dubious gambler's trade. He'd bought himself a vest of milk-white cloth, sewn with gold brocade, and when he wore it he could not be beaten, and the image of the yellow-haired prince stayed in his mind, more powerful than a memory, as if the prince were still seeking his help.

As for Lucas, he too felt the spirit of the fog, especially in the part of town that held the theatres; when he dropped a fare off on Player Street at curtain time he would be seized by an intense hunger for cream of potato soup. Outside the Maiden Theatre he actually had the flavor of it on his tongue, as the mist danced about his cab and touched his lips. "He's near," said Lucas to himself. "He's hangin' about."

When this experience repeated itself many nights in a row, Lucas took himself to the Casino Mundo, found Erlwine at the gaming table, and made a report. "The Maiden Theatre, Erlwine, that's where he's at, right now."

Erlwine cashed in, and he and Lucas rode to Player Street, Erlwine seated beside Lucas on the cabman's seat, both men listening to the melancholy sound of iron hooves on stone echoing in a narrow lane. "All the city's secrets—" Lucas flicked his whip lightly in the air. "—the cobbles know more than you and me."

They crossed the city from waterfront to Player Street, and at the Maiden Theatre the fog was alive, swirling with unnatural agitation, ducking into cracks in doors and windows and rolling along the courtyard that led to the stagedoor.

The play was nearly done, and Erlwine and Lucas were able to enter unnoticed; onstage was Belle Nugent in her last scene. Lucas pointed with his whip to a box seat above the stage, where a misty figure sat in ghostly evening wear, gaze fixed upon the young actress. "So that's it," growled Lucas under his breath.

Erlwine nodded. Prince Nimbus was in love with Belle Nugent, was risking his kingdom for her. It seemed extreme. But then, thought Erlwine, Prince Nimbus is a gambler.

The play concluded and Belle Nugent took her bows. Prince Nimbus tossed a misty rose toward the

stage. It descended slowly, blended with the smoke that danced in the footlights and was lost. Nimbus turned and vanished from his box.

"The stagedoor," said Erlwine, and he and Lucas made their way to it, and waited there in the crowd. Presently, veiled within sheets of mist that had fallen on the courtyard, a figure appeared in the crowd, hat in hand, pacing nervously. Only Lucas and Erlwine perceived the prince; to other eyes it seemed that the mist was thicker than usual, and agitated by a restless breeze playing along the courtyard. But when Belle Nugent made her exit from the theatre, both mist and men were disturbed.

"Miss Nugent, your autograph, please!"

"Dear Miss Nugent, could you—would you—"

She paused briefly, with professional smiles and pleasantries, and then her leading man in the play helped her into her carriage; she drew her rustling skirts in, and he climbed in beside her. The cabman flicked his reins.

"She's gone, Prince," said Erlwine softly.

"To whom are you speaking, sir?" asked another gentleman; he didn't see Prince Nimbus, saw only fog sinking along the bricks of the theatre.

"Steady, steady," said Lucas, keeping Prince Nimbus upright.

"The pair of them, out of their head," muttered the gentleman, and watched as Erlwine and Lucas put their arms through fog and walked away as if supporting someone between them.

"I have fallen from the clouds for her," said Nimbus, the music gone from his voice, his words now like the hissing of a gas jet in the fog. His elegant form was no longer princely; he stared like a dog after Belle Nugent's carriage as it rattled off into the night.

"We'd best follow," said Lucas, and showed the way to his own carriage. Erlwine and the prince settled into the soft leather seats of the Diligence. The prince might have been any young fool smitten by love, except for this: a misty face attended him, swirling outside the carriage—his sorceror, Stilla Galbanum, trying to protect him on his foolish errand.

"Her voice, my friend," said the prince to Erlwine. "Have you heard her voice, so rich and deep, as if wrapped in delicate fog?"

"We'll bring you through this, Prince." Erlwine's thumb was hooked inside his gold watch chain; he was confident, was on a winning streak. What was love? Just a game of cards.

Lucas, in the driver's seat, was having his own conversation with Stilla Galbanum; the sorceror's form was less distinct than the prince's, was a foggy shroud in which two eyes gleamed. "Soon we will not be able to bring him back," said Stilla Galbanum, shaking his head.

Lucas held the reins lightly, his eyes on the carriage in front of them, where Belle Nugent rode with her leading man. She don't even know our prince exists, thought Lucas to himself. And if she did? He's a nice enough feller but he's got no weight to him. Some of my soup's what he needs. Put the iron into his veins.

"That solution is not suitable," said the thought-reading sorceror. "The prince cannot take on substance. He will, in fact, soon be scattered like the ordinary mist and his noble line will come to an end."

"Well, why don't you fix him up with a girl from his own world?" Lucas pointed his whip upward. "Ain't you got any around?"

"There is no one whose stars are in the appropriate place."

"Hang the stars," said Lucas. "She's just got to have a bit of zip in her, that's all, like Miss Nugent." He pointed with the other end of his whip. "For that's apparently what he favors."

"I appreciate your concern," said the sorceror, but his presence grew noticeably chillier, so much so that Lucas had to wrap a blanket around himself.

"You're goin' to have a prince got no more life in him than a puff of steam over a teapot."

"I am Stilla Galbanum, Master of Spells. I can handle the situation."

"And what happens, Gab'num, if the prince goes up the flue?"

"A new prince will be crowned."

"Got somebody lined up, do you?"

"That is a secret of the court."

"Wouldn't be yourself, by any chance, would it?"

Stilla Galbanum, Master of Spells, vanished.

Lucas kept pace with Belle Nugent's carriage, though he knew now that it was hopeless, owing to the prince's inability to take soup and gain weight. Belle Nugent's carriage stopped at Casino Mundo. Lucas's own carriage door opened and Prince Nimbus leapt out.

Nimbus ran after the actress, reached for her. She felt nothing, it was only fog at her shoulder. Nimbus raced to the door of the casino and threw himself down before her.

Belle Nugent walked over Prince Nimbus, one glittering shoe tip piercing his heart, while the sweep of her long skirt scattered the rest of him to either side of the doorway.

"He is dead!" cried Stilla Galbanum, appearing at the doorway.

"Not yet," said Lucas, and he and Erlwine did that most difficult thing, they held the fog in their hands, and shaped it, gathering Prince Nimbus together by the strength of their affection for him, for he was the harvest color moon, he was love dying in the dark, and they could not let that happen. They carried him back to the carriage, bundled him inside, and took him away.

Lucas opened the sliding panel that gave into the carriage. "You've no friend in that Gab'nun feller, Prince."

"What does it matter?" groaned Nimbus. "Belle Nugent will never be mine."

"There are other queens in the pack," said Erlwine, and then called to Lucas through the open panel. "Take us to some den."

"Aye," said Lucas.

They sat in a dark corner of the cabman's cafe Lucas had found, where a bit of fog at a table simply blended with the smoke that wreathed the room. Lucas and Erlwine made the prince swallow the steam from some mulled cider. "That'll put the whipcrack back in you, Prince," said Lucas. "Drink it down."

"She never saw me," sighed Nimbus.

"No, and she never will," said Lucas. "You and her don't mix well, lad."

"Why?" cried Nimbus.

"It's the way of things," said Lucas. "Now, let's get practical. Are there any chances of your findin' a young lady of your own sort?"

"Where, in heaven's name?" Prince Nimbus threw back the evening cape from his shoulders, spread his arms out wide, hands questioning. "The clouds are empty, and Stilla Galbanum says there's no hope of finding a girl of the mist on earth."

"He said that, did he? He said there was no hope down here?" Lucas looked at the prince sharply, then turned his gaze to Erlwine.

The gambler ran his fingers along his gold watch chain. "Now," he said, "I feel the cards changing."

They walked among the closed fruit stalls, where a few battered fruits still lay on the ground. Lucas picked up a pomegranate which had fallen behind a stall. Its seeds glittered in his hand. "They calls this the apple of love, Prince. It's a good sign for us now, don't you think?" But even as he held it out to the prince, a swirling little cloud of cold fell on it, and covered it with frost. "Your friend Gas'bun is followin' us."

"I can trust no one," sighed the prince.

"You can trust Erlwine," said Lucas. "And you can trust me."

"Had I any power left, I'd reward you, but I've lost my command. I've spent myself on folly."

Erlwine smiled. "What man hasn't?"

"That's right," said Lucas. "We're all a bunch of fools out here in the dark. What we got to do, Prince, see—" He made a figure-eight design in the air with his whip. "—is weave. Weave through the night. That's the cabman's way. And he always finds a fare."

After the fruit stalls came an arcade, with fortune-tellers, shooting galleries. Erlwine showed his skill with a rifle, blasting rows of tin ducks, and Prince Nimbus tried to give his misty hand to a palmist, but she said she wouldn't read palms for ghosts.

"I'm not a ghost, madame. I'm an elemental."

"Oh, all right, let me see . . . ah, someone's been walking on your heart line."

"Put a shoe through it," said Lucas. "Pretty near killed him, did Miss Belle Nugent."

"Keep good friends with you, you need them now. To outwit a powerful adversary—" She drew her fingers suddenly away. "Your hand is ice! I'm frozen!" She held up frost-covered fingertips.

"Gas'bum!" Lucas thrashed around them, but the sorceror had withdrawn and the palmist was howling with pain as the blood came back to her fingers. Prince Nimbus tried to pay her with a misty coin, but she said, "I don't go shopping in the clouds," and shooed him away, along with Lucas.

Erlwine joined them, carrying a paper bird on a

stick he'd won. They attached it to the cab, where it fluttered its wings as they rode along to a noisy street whose factories ran night and day. Looms were clattering and workers' voices could be heard dimly beneath the noise. The windows were lit but were so smudged and dark one could not see in. "Still," said Lucas, "feel the goin's-on, Prince. It's what I do of an evenin' when I have no fare. I park here, and listen. I listen."

Lucas's eyes were bright and Erlwine felt the night was coming toward them. Someone, or something, was wrapped in it. "A good hand builds slowly," he said to Prince Nimbus, who gazed in confusion toward the factory window and the clatter of the loom.

"Listen," said Lucas. "It says, weave, weave."

They moved on, but upon the factory windows there was left an unnatural trace of frost.

Lucas led them through other neighborhoods he knew, some carefully tended and housing lovely gardens, others ruined and broken, with windows boarded over and roofs falling off. Prince Nimbus knew none of it, except in a vague way, for earth to him was as the dream world is to us—a place not quite real, not quite graspable, and liable to dissolve at any moment. The strain of staying so long in this earthly realm was showing—his hat kept floating off, and the edges of his cape unraveled, escaping into the fog. "Hold fast to him, Erlwine, or he'll leak away on us."

Erlwine forced the prince to concentrate, on cards,

on tricks, on sleights of hand. By the dim lantern light of the carriage he showed Nimbus how ace, king, queen, and knave could weave through a pack, to a place one could always find, ". . . like this, Prince, there you are . . . didn't expect that one, did you . . ." and so forth, and the prince held his shape, which is not easy when your head is tending to drift, and your feet are going through the floor, and a sorceror named Stilla Galbanum from the clouds is making spells designed to hasten your dissolution.

They wove through the city, from its bright center of a thousand gaslights to its dark fringes where only a campfire burned by the river, tended by some shadowy traveler forgotten by the world.

"It's hopeless," said Prince Nimbus, gazing out the carriage window at the black river. "Let me disintegrate. I shall become the unformed mist curling about the rooftops."

Yes, whispered Stilla Galbanum, *how peaceful to slip along the windowpanes, and forget . . .*

"Git! Git! You sneaky devil!" Lucas cracked his whip at the shape of Galbanum, but the sorceror divided where the whip struck him.

I should be a better ruler, said Galbanum.

Lucas stopped the carriage. They were in a field by the river, and the road was just a mud track used by fishermen's carts, to and from the shore. Erlwine climbed out, with the prince beside him. "I can hold him no longer," said Erlwine.

The prince's face was fading, his features less distinguishable every moment. "Thank you, my friends," he said. "I shall leave you here."

Come away, said Stilla Galbanum. *How peaceful is the mist . . .*

Prince Nimbus walked solemnly toward the river, his form dissolving slowly.

"I took him as far as a cabman can," said Lucas, voice catching in his throat. "Ain't that right, boys?" Lucas patted the steaming flanks of his horses. The horses' steam rose up, blending with the slowly rolling fog off the river; to it was added a part of the smoke of the lonely traveler's distant campfire; and a bit of vapor from the carriage lantern completed the blend. Erlwine acted fast, with the only strength he had—he whipped out his deck of cards and fanned it at the misty blend, and the tiny breeze from the cards' fluttering edges held the vapor intact.

Lucas grabbed his whip, and grabbed the paper bird on the stick as well, and then, like a lunatic, danced around the vapor, cracking his whip and fluttering the bird under, around, and above the blended mist. It is not what men do but how they do it, and Erlwine and Lucas were shouting and prancing, fanning and dancing with all their hearts, for it was all they had there on the forlorn river bank. The vapor held. And four tiny queens were fanning off the slick surface of Erlwine's cards; their heads were lifting, then their arms and legs, and suddenly they were loose and floating in the air, bright inks set free in liquid shimmering color. They floated toward the column of smoke and steam, and then, with a sudden rush, imprinted themselves upon it.

"Luck has changed!" shouted Erlwine, staring at

the now brightly colored vapor, which suddenly had a character, that of fortune, the queens of chance.

"That's got it, Erlwine!" Lucas was cracking his whip and waving his bird on a stick, and Stilla Galbanum, unable to resist an incantation, threw his own force into the works.

"Merge!" he shouted, and the four queens did, sinking toward the center of the shimmering mist. It whorled in a wild spiral and when it stopped she appeared—a young woman of the same substance as Prince Nimbus.

Nimbus, on the edge of dissolution, turned. He saw the misty girl, and love burst in his heart.

He went toward her, a bit of his fog hat in his hands, and then the rest of it reappearing as he drew his form together again. His cape shone. He spoke to her softly.

"Hmmmmfff," sniffed Stilla Galbanum.

"We done it, Erlwine," said Lucas.

The prince and the magic girl were left alone by the others, and Nimbus showed her things a prince can do when he remembers who he is—shaping the mist into flowers for her hair, shaping a cloak, a necklace of dewdrops, a ring of misty moonstones. He was Stilla Galbanum's student, after all, and a few more passes of his hands created a little boat from the mist, and into it he stepped, and helped her in after him. The prince rowed with two shafts of moonlight. The magic girl sat across from him, and leaning back she saw that his hair was like the yellow harvest moon, which enchants all who fall within its rays.

Lucas, Erlwine, and Stilla Galbanum watched from the shore. "But will he be able to return to his home?" asked Lucas with a cabman's concern. "For I could make another flyin' run at the pier." He pointed to his carriage.

"He made a boat," said Stilla Galbanum. "He can make a carriage too. He can make little planets, sun, and moons. The prince is now king."

Lucas looked at the sorceror, whose misty edges were swirling restlessly. "Guess you'll be out of a job, Gas'num."

"True, a misplayed hand."

"What'll you do?"

"Oh, a sorceror always has a home." Galbanum bowed his shrouded head. His eyes had pupils with rings around them, as does the orb of Saturn. He faded, and was gone.

Erlwine and Lucas stepped toward the carriage, and climbed up together to the seat. The horses started on their own, along the muddy fisherman's road, and Lucas took the carriage slowly back to the cobbled pathways, where sleek evening carriages carried passengers of every sort. The heart of town was blazing, lanterns lit up and down the streets and avenues. The Diligence mixed in among them, and soon was lost in the brilliant traffic of those who enjoy the night.

∽   ∽   ∽

I waited, but nothing more came. The story of the Diligence was ended, the rest of the page remaining blank before me. I got up, walked to the window, looked out into the darkness. The moon had gone behind a cloud, illuminating its edges. Somewhere beyond it was the castle of Prince Nimbus, I was sure. I stood there for a long time, just staring into the sky. My back was stiff, my shoulders tired. Now, perhaps, I might be able to go to bed.

But then I heard, as if from somewhere deep inside my mind, the roaring of a jungle animal. And faintly, the blowing of a bugle. I returned to the desk, and turned to a new page in the empty notebook . . .

Fourth Tale

From the Empty Notebook

The Tiger's Tail

The back stairs were always locked. "They only go to the attic," said Mother. "And there's nothing up there but a lot of tired furniture."

"Why is it tired?" asked Angela.

"Any suits of armor?" asked Adrian.

"Of course not," said Mother. "What kind of attic do you think we have?"

"We'll never know until you let us up there."

"It's damp and stuffy and not suitable."

"Not suitable," said Adrian, when he and Angela were alone. "You know what that means."

"It must be the best room in the house."

They knew all about the den with its ancient firearms, and the library with its wallsafe hidden by a row of dusty books. They knew about the cool rooms of the wine cellar, and the cavern of the dumb-waiter, down which Adrian had once lowered Angela, which gave Cook a terrible surprise. They knew all about the old house—except for the back staircase leading to the attic.

"You see," Adrian explained to Angela when they had stolen the key and were on their way toward the staircase, "Mother and Father think it's just an old staircase. They can't see the mystery."

"Well, maybe there is no mystery."

"You know better than that, Angela. There's always mystery in locked-up things."

"Yes," said Angela, "but maybe when we unlock it, there'll be no more mystery, and even if there is, we'll still be in trouble with Mother."

"She's not going to find out."

"Didn't she find out about the dumbwaiter?"

"Only because Cook thought you were a burglar."

"I *said*, 'Quiet, Cook, it's only me.' "

"Yes, but she couldn't see it was only you. You should have given her a code word."

"Well, I couldn't think of one."

"I gave you plenty of them. Didn't I write them on your sleeve?"

"It's too dark to read a sleeve in a dumbwaiter, and you should have thought of that, Adrian, if you're so smart."

"Let's not quarrel, shall we?" Adrian held up the key. "Mother's out shopping and Cook is asleep in her room. We'll never have a better chance than now."

They went quietly past the library, to the locked door at the rear of the downstairs hall. Adrian slipped the key into the lock, and the door creaked slowly open. He waved his sister in after him, and they started up the stairs.

"It's drafty, just like Mother said." Angela put her finger through a cobweb. "And dusty too."

"Of course it's dusty," said Adrian. "Nobody ever cleans it. It's sealed off, like the Pharaoh's tomb."

"Do you have to make it scarier than it already is?"

"Yes," said Adrian. "I do."

"Well, it's horrid of you."

"Angela, I'm perfectly happy to continue on alone."

"Don't be so pompous. I hate it when you're pompous."

"Well, don't you be timorous."

"I'm not timorous." Angela's footsteps were right behind her brother's. "I'm cautious."

Adrian turned the first landing; the only light was from a small square window above the landing, and it was covered from outside by dead leaves, which cast ragged shadows on the floor. "It's exactly like the Pharaoh's tomb. Can't you feel the dark influences?"

"I feel a lot of nasty cobwebs in my hair."

"Those *are* the dark influences, Angela."

"Well, I hope you like them, because I don't."

"We couldn't ask for darker influences than these, Angela. The back staircase is everything we'd hoped for."

"I never hoped for a lot of nasty cobwebs."

"You can't enter the Pharaoh's antechamber without some cobwebs, and I, for one, am thankful."

Adrian brushed a cobweb off his face, and tossed it aside with great relish.

"Adrian, you flung that right in my hair!"

"Didn't see you."

"Well, I'm right in back of you."

They continued up the next flight of stairs, Adrian taking care not to throw cobwebs in Angela's face, though it was great fun to dash them aside with one clean sweep of his arm. "I wish we had a torch."

"Mother wouldn't like us lighting torches in the house, Adrian."

"Angela, I want to tell you something." Adrian turned dramatically on the stair. "I don't believe we're in our house any longer."

"We're not? Then where are we?"

"We're in another dimension. I felt us going through as we turned that landing."

"Well, if it's another dimension, how is it that I can hear Cook snoring through the wall?"

Adrian paused, and cocked his ear in the direction Angela was pointing. "The spirit of the Pharaoh's sacred cow is snorting," said Adrian. "They're put into the tomb with him, you know."

"That's Cook, Adrian. Her room is just beyond this wall."

"Her room *would* be beyond this wall, if we hadn't changed dimensions. No, Angela, I hate to disappoint you, but that is not Cook we're hearing, but the Pharaoh's own sacred cow, whose horns are tipped with gold."

"Well, the Pharaoh's cow is muttering in her sleep about *our* supper."

"Angela, if you spoil this game, I'll tie you up and tickle you until you scream."

"You just try it."

They continued to the next landing, where the light again fell in dim, ragged beams onto the dusty stairs. "One more flight," said Adrian, "and we'll be there."

"Where will we be?"

"At the heart of the mystery," said Adrian softly, and led the way. "There's liable to be danger."

"In our own attic?"

"If only it were our own attic," said Adrian.

"You were expecting it to be someone else's attic?"

"I don't know what to expect," said Adrian. "But I'm absolutely certain it will be unlike anything we've ever dreamed of."

The last turning in the stair was a short one, and just five steps above them was a dark expanse of sloping roof. They crested the stairs, and stepped out onto the attic floor. Light from a series of small dormer windows fell in little rectangles along a seemingly endless corridor. On all sides of this corridor furniture was piled—and old bicycles, wagons, sleds, and skis. There were countless trunks, and stacks of wooden tea chests. There were lamps, and birdbaths, statues, and rugs. As far as the eye could see, all this was duplicated, again and again, creating a gigantic maze.

"It's greater than the Pharaoh's tomb!" cried Adrian.

"It certainly is a jumble," said Angela.

"We crossed dimensions, Angela. I told you we did."

"It's funny we didn't feel anything. Just Cook's snoring was all."

"Let's explore!"

"Look at all this lovely furniture. A very nice little parlor could be made."

"I don't have time for that. We've got to see how far it goes!"

"Well, you go and report back," said Angela. "I think I'll stay right here."

"Afraid?"

"I'm quite comfortable, actually, and I intend to make some tasteful arrangements."

"Seems like a waste to me."

"Yes, I suppose it must." Angela was looking about for a nice cleared space in which to do some arranging, and spied an alcove, just ahead of her, completely empty, with streams of dusty sunlight coming into it. "There's the perfect place. It's going to be my new room, and I'll come here whenever I want to ponder."

"You're dotty," said Adrian. "There's adventure here." He pointed down the long corridor.

"Run along, Adrian. If you get into trouble, give a yell."

"A lot of good yelling will do, if I'm bound and gagged."

"Are you planning on being bound and gagged?"

"One doesn't *plan* on being bound and gagged, Angela. Dark hands simply reach out, pinion you in spite of your struggles, and then you're never heard from again."

"I'm quite certain I'll be hearing from you again, Adrian."

"Are you? Do you think whoever put this monumental amount of stuff up here has left it unguarded? Do you think we plunge ahead into nothing but a lot of couches?"

"I'm plunging into this one," said Angela, and pulled out the end of a mahogany framed sofa with velvet cushions. "It will be the centerpiece of my room."

"Farewell, Angela. You may stay here and arrange furniture if you like. I must push on."

"First, push on the end of this couch. Thank you. And now could you help me with— "

"I didn't steal the key and risk all in order to decorate an alcove. Goodbye, dear sister. If you should be attacked, scream and I'll come running—if I'm able to."

Angela had stopped listening to her brother. She was putting a bamboo tea table into place in front of the couch. "There, that's a very nice effect, don't you think? Adrian?" She turned, but there was no sign of her brother, which did not particularly bother her, because Adrian's only use for furniture was jumping up and down on it pretending to swordfight. "He'd just wreck my arrangement," she said to herself, as she swung a 17th century daybed into place, near the couch.

"It's just the thing for me to read a book on, and over here I shall put this straight ladderback chair, not very comfortable, and that'll be for Adrian, *if* I even let him in my room, which is doubtful, because he'll only start a swordfight and topple the tea table. Now, what else?" She arranged an oak writing desk, with an oak chair to match it. "Here is where I'll keep my diary, and my infamous memoirs. Oh, and look at this!" She dusted off a three-seated chair, one which allowed three people to sit at angles to each other, shoulders almost touching. "That is so cozy, it practically cries out for a cat to grace it, deep in the cushions." She turned to put a music stand into place, and when she turned back, a cat was curled up deep in the cushions, looking at her.

"Where did you come from? Are you the attic mouser?" She brushed her hand over the cat's soft fur, and felt it purring beneath her touch. "I shall call you Pharaoh, in deference to my brother, who *did* steal the key to the attic. When he's sitting uncomfortably in the ladderback chair, you jump on his lap to console him."

Pharaoh began to wash. "Which reminds me," said Angela, "one must have a washstand, for not all of us can clean up with our tongue." She searched along the row of piled furniture and found a washstand which was decorated with inlaid birds and flowers, and she moved it into place. "And now, for a tea set." She found a teapot, and a jam pot, and a cake basket, all in silver. Then came silver forks, knives, and spoons with seashells etched upon their handles. She added plates and cups and saucers, which bore brightly painted scenes.

She arranged all of the crockery very carefully, and

each thing gave her a strange and special feeling—as if the furniture and the dishes and the silver tea set had memories of their own, memories that reached out and touched her, with hints and whispers concerning their long history. When she sat down upon her three-seated chair, beside Pharaoh the cat, it was with an odd sense that she knew something just beyond the edges of her thought—something old and indescribably lovely.

Adrian tracked along through each row of high stacked trunks and dangling sleds. He touched nothing. There would always be time for that. The important thing was to explore it all, to map it out and determine its full extent. That was the proper work of an explorer. So, though there were many, many games and toys of every kind piled up, he let them be. He loved the display, and the vastness of it all. It made his soul sing out to see so many corridors, so many niches, so many stacks of furniture clear to the dark ceiling. "I always knew a place like this existed," he said to himself as he walked along. "I've dreamt of it, but it was a dream so deep that I could never remember it on waking. I wonder if Angela has dreamt it too?" He looked back up the main corridor, but he could no longer see exactly where it was he'd left her. "Angela, can you hear me?"

No answer came. "She's probably bound and gagged already." He continued along through the shadowy aisles, amidst beds, desks, billiard tables, clocks, umbrella stands, and a thousand other things. "Hello, what's that?"

Something had moved, up ahead, from one aisle to the next. Adrian crept slowly forward, and waited. He heard someone humming! A chill ran through him at the thought that their very own attic was not their very own. The humming came closer, and a small, grizzled man turned the corner. His pants were baggy, his hair askew, and he had the look of a crack-brained old parrot. Adrian drew himself to his full height, which made him almost as tall as the man, and said, "Who are you?"

"Pinover's the name," said the man. "Who are you?"

"I live downstairs."

"I never go there," said Pinover, with perfect assurance, and Adrian had the feeling that Mr. Pinover considered the downstairs part of the house beneath him, in more ways than one.

"Well," said Adrian, trying to assume the air of the young master of the house, including the attic, "what exactly do you do up here?"

"Do? I live here, that's what I do. What are you doing here?"

"I'm—exploring," said Adrian, his confidence waning again.

"Plenty to see," said Pinover. "Come on, I'll show you." He led Adrian into the next aisle, which, like so many of the other aisles, was filled with heavy furniture, stacked to the roof. "That's the way I like it—stacked," said Pinover. "Now there's a lovely show of legs—" He pointed to a tower of chairs, the legs all nested, chair upon chair.

"Yes," said Adrian, much confused, "it's all quite—wedged."

"Stacked and wedged, there you have it. Of course, there's always room for a bit more."

The baggy-pantsed old fellow led on to the next aisle, where more furniture and some decorative fish nets were stored. "Lovely stuff," said the man. "And plenty more just like it." He led them back out of the aisle.

"Look down the main corridor, my boy. Look straight down there—"

The old crank pointed, and Adrian looked down a corridor lined with mirrors for as far as the eye could see.

"Those mirrors," said Pinover, "are the cause of enormous mischief to somebody trying to find their way. Mirrors should be arranged differently, with the glass facing in, so as not to trouble the eye. But some imbecile put them with the glass facing out. In consequence of which, a man can't always get his bearings."

"But the attic door is just—" Adrian turned to point toward it, and found himself unable to recognize anything, except his own face reflected in a series of mirrors.

"Angela! Angela, where are you!"

Angela stood in the center of her alcove, with everything in place. The furniture was arranged, and the tea set was out. All was in readiness for visitors. She sat down on the sofa, across from Pharaoh, and snapped open a Chinese fan she'd found.

She heard the lightest of footsteps approaching. Turning, she saw a little roly-poly woman entering, an umbrella over her arm, a flowered hat on her head, and a handbag in her hand. "Well," said the woman, "you've shifted things."

"Yes," said Angela, "I hope that's all right?"

"Of course it's all right. It would be all right if you dynamited it." The woman plopped down on the daybed. "It would give a person room to maneuver."

"It is awfully jammed-in up here."

"What's your name?"

"Angela."

"Mine's Ginger. I used to be in theatricals."

"Really? And how did you get into our attic?"

"Your attic? I like that. Do you spend your days walking from aisle to aisle? Do you sleep on a pile of mattresses up which you have to climb with a ladder?"

"I'm sorry, I didn't mean to be—proprietary."

Ginger lifted an eyebrow. "Don't use fancy words on me, young lady. I'm a good deal older than you are."

"I just meant—I'm glad you're in our attic. It makes it much more fun."

"Fun? You call this fun?" Ginger removed her shoe and wiggled her toes. "I've been walking for hours."

"Where were you headed for?"

"Right here, dearie, to your nice daybed." Ginger kicked her other shoe off and stretched out, wiggling both sets of toes. She looked around the pleasant little alcove, which Angela had so carefully arranged.

"Such a relief to be where there's only one of a thing. One chair, one sofa, one whatever-that-is."

"I think it's a three-seated chair."

Pharaoh looked up from his part of the three-seated chair, and Ginger said, "I see *he's* made himself comfortable."

"Yes, isn't he lovely? Do you know him?"

"We meet from time to time." Ginger eyed the cat. "I suppose you wish I carried dried fish in my purse." Ginger turned back toward Angela. "I don't though."

"Don't what?"

"Carry dried fish in my purse. Do you?"

"No, of course not."

"Just checking." Ginger removed her hat and set it on the tea table. "How old are you?"

"Ten."

"First time up the attic?"

"We had to steal the key."

"We?"

"Adrian and I. He's my brother."

"Probably off exploring."

"How did you know?"

"He'll be lost in no time flat."

"Oh dear," said Angela. "Will he be able to find his way back?"

"I doubt it."

"Well, we should go and look for him!" Angela rose from her seat.

"Unless he meets—" Ginger turned her head slightly, and spoke from the side of her mouth. "—the old buzzard."

"Who is that?"

"Just an old buzzard." Ginger laid her umbrella down against the daybed. "Don't worry about your brother."

Angela sat back down, and returned her gaze to Ginger. "Have you been up the attic long?"

"Long enough. Don't have a cigar on you, do you?"

"No, I'm afraid I don't."

"A proper young lady. I was just checking." Ginger continued wriggling her toes. "I walked my dogs off."

"Do you spend a lot of time—walking?"

"Today I found the carpets. Had to crawl over about a hundred of them. You could use a carpet in here." Ginger pointed to the area beneath the tea table. "A little one, right there."

"That would be grand."

"We'll find one in a minute. After my dogs cool off."

"I'm sorry your—dogs are hurting, Ginger."

"Not as sorry as I am." Ginger rubbed her ankle, gave a long sigh, and then stood up in her stocking feet. "All right, young lady, let's get you a carpet."

"Will we have to go far?"

"I doubt it." They walked to the edge of the alcove and Ginger peered between two bookcases. "Stick your arm in there."

Angela did as she was told, and came out with a small Oriental carpet, very thick and covered with bright flowers. "It's a dear little carpet."

"It'll do." Ginger helped move the tea table, and they placed the carpet under it, so that it was directly in front of the sofa. Ginger sat down on the sofa, and rubbed her feet back and forth over the thickly woven flowers on the carpet's face. "Very cozy. Just what we needed. I'll drop in here on my rounds each day, and rest my dogs while we have a chat."

"That would be nice," said Angela. "And you could tell me about your theatricals."

"I played tree stumps mostly. Talking tree stumps. Because of my height."

"You *are* short."

"I fit in a tree stump nicely."

"I can see how you would." Angela sat down next to Ginger on the sofa. "I'd like to write a theatrical someday."

"Put a tree stump in it."

"I certainly will."

"You're a fine young lady." Ginger touched at her hair. "Speaking of dried fish—"

Angela looked up, startled. "Were we speaking of dried fish?"

"I don't suppose you get much of it downstairs?"

"Occasionally we do."

"I was thinking more of the cat than myself." Ginger nodded at Pharaoh, who looked back at her suspiciously, as if not quite believing that she was looking out for his needs alone.

"Yes," continued Ginger, "he likes a bit of dried fish now and then. It can be very tasty. He likes cheese with it too."

"Well, I shall be sure to bring some up for him."

"If you set it on this tea table here, I'm sure he'll find it," said Ginger. "You should cover it securely though, so flies don't get at it."

Pharaoh's eyes became two slits, as he gazed at Ginger.

"I'll put it down in a silver serving bowl with a silver lid," said Angela.

"That's a good girl. Around eight o'clock every morning. With a pot of hot tea."

"Does the cat like hot tea?"

"Adores it. With cream and sugar."

"What an unusual cat."

"Unpredictable creatures," said Ginger. "Some of them even fancy buttered toast. We *could* try it on him, and see if he likes it."

"Perhaps I should make a list," said Angela.

"Good idea." Ginger snapped open her purse, and took out a little silver pencil and a tiny notebook. "I'll just jot the items down—" Ginger concentrated, the tip of her tongue peeking out of the corner of her mouth as she wrote. "There, that should do it." She tore the page from her notebook and handed it to Angela. "A cat would be very happy with a menu like that."

"Would you—I mean would the cat—like a poached egg too?"

"Lovely, dearie, just lovely. Well, I suppose I should put my shoes back on and go."

"Where are you headed for?"

"Oh, I just point my umbrella."

"Does it ever rain in the attic?"

"Leaky roof." Ginger pointed with the tip. "I don't like to get wet."

"Nor do I."

"Well, there are lots of umbrellas scattered around up here." Ginger put on her shoes.

"Couldn't you stay a bit longer?"

"What would we do?"

"You could show me how to be a tree stump."

"All right, it's a golden opportunity for you to learn. Come and stand over here, that's it—"

"I wish Adrian were here to learn. Being a tree stump is just the kind of thing he would like."

Adrian, however, was rushing up and down through the aisles of furniture, looking for a familiar landmark. "Oh, why do all old chests of drawers look the same?"

"A question I've asked often through the years," said Pinover, scuttling along directly behind Adrian.

"It's a regular jungle."

"Stuffed animals."

"Really?"

"Yes, and they can give you an awful fright at nightfall, with their glass eyes glowing at the end of some quiet row. Twist you right around in your shoes, they will."

Adrian climbed up a tower of chairs, to the very top, where he knelt, the tower swaying beneath him.

"See anything?"

"It goes on—forever."

"Any sign of marmalade?"

"Marmalade?"

"Comes in a jar, tastes quite sweet?"

"I *know* what marmalade is."

"Good. Can you see any?"

"No."

"Sometimes you run across it out here. Whole shelves of it."

Adrian looked down at the old coot, who was bracing the tower of chairs with his foot, and had resumed his humming. He looked up at Adrian. "Mind you don't shift that pile of love seats alongside you. Nothing worse than being crushed under an avalanche of love seats."

"I'm being careful," said Adrian, as he lowered himself slowly, rung by rung, down the tower of chairs.

"You're a spry lad," said the old veteran of the attic, as Adrian landed on the floor beside him. "Like your Dad before you."

"Do you know my Dad?"

"Knew him when he was a boy. He's long forgot me now."

"I'm sure he wouldn't forget that he had someone living in his attic," said Adrian.

"No, they get to a certain age and they forget. Your grandfather was the same."

"My grandfather? You knew grandfather too?"

Mr. Pinover's eyes took on a bright, conspiratorial sparkle. "He supplied me with marmalade. And tinned biscuits. I had it quite comfortable up here all the time your granddad was a boy. But then he grew up, and I sort of faded from his mind."

"How very sad."

"I went on short rations then. Had to hunt up my own tinned biscuits and marmalade. Now I don't say you can't find them here, you can, but it's a great pleasure to have them brought to you."

"Grandfather never came here after he grew up?"

"I observed him from afar. Crouched in a pile of sinks, you see. He never saw me. He had a different look in his eye. And—no marmalade."

"I'm terribly sorry."

"A man can't last long without marmalade."

"Yes, of course."

"You get dry as a stuffed hen. Dust starts to settle on you, and the next thing you know, you're an exhibit." The old crank shook out the lapels of his jacket. "Fortunately for me, your Dad came along, discovered me here, and put me back on rations. Some of the finest marmalade I ever had. On the tangy side. He was just about the age you are now."

"How very odd."

"It's the pattern. There's a pattern to things." Pinover looked at Adrian, his eyes twinkling once again. "A pattern, don't you see."

"I'm not quite sure—"

"Next time you're having some marmalade—"

"I'll bring you some!"

"Now you've got it."

"But," said Adrian, "I can't bring you marmalade if I never find my way back to the attic door."

"Map."

"You've got one?"

"Been workin' on it for some time." Pinover took out a pile of wrinkled pieces of paper from his vest and spread one of them open on a desk top. "Now, let's see, where in thunder are we? Hmmmmmmnn.

Here's the pile of dwarf bookcases, and over there should be the stack of sleds. Am I right?"

Adrian saw the low row of miniature bookcases, and opposite them, a tangle of old curling runners. "Yes sir, they're there."

"Good." Pinover folded his map. "Then we're completely lost."

"What do you mean?"

"It means I'm at the edge of my map. I haven't worked it up one pace further than this."

"But why not?"

"Lack of marmalade."

"I shall lead us back," said Adrian. "I know I can do it."

"I have every faith in you myself, because you most likely had some marmalade quite recently."

"As a matter of fact, for breakfast."

"With buttered toast?"

"Yes."

"Lead on."

Adrian led on, with Pinover following close behind him.

"You'd have no objection, I suppose, if I blew a bugle?" The old crackpot reached up for one which dangled overhead. He put the mouthpiece to his lips and blew, and a feeble, sputtering sound came out the other end. "Must be plugged up inside," he said, shaking it, and a mouse fell out, and scurried away. "Now you'll hear some bugling," he said, and blew again. A second sputtering sound emerged. He looked at Adrian. "Lack of marmalade. Affects the wind."

Adrian pressed on, taking what felt like the correct turning. They wound up in a dead end, formed by stacks of old newspapers which towered to the sloping roof. "I'm sorry," said Adrian, as they backtracked out of the cul-de-sac.

"Yes, it's all so familiar," said Pinover. "And yet—where are we?"

"Well, we're *somewhere* in the attic."

"A bloodhound would be the beast we'd need, but—" Pinover held a finger in the air. "—he'd be a drain on the biscuit."

"I shall lead us out," said Adrian. "The important thing is not to panic."

"Right, we can always sleep in a drawer."

"I have no intention of spending the night here," said Adrian, and led on, past old rocking horses and playpens, archery sets and targets, and an upright piano. "But where did it all come from?" he wondered to himself.

"Had signs been provided—biscuit here, marmalade there—but no." Pinover was opening and closing a series of drawers, along a row of bureaus. "But it's treasure, my lad, treasure all the same, every last stick of it."

"I guess you must like it up here."

"Well, it's home, you see."

"We never hear you downstairs."

"I don't like to make a fuss."

"But your trumpet. I mean, when you've had enough marmalade and you blow it—"

"Sound is muffled," said Pinover. "Caught and suppressed by the innumerable wads of junk."

"Look!" said Adrian, pointing ahead. "That umbrella stand!"

"Could be any one of five thousand or so."

"There was one right near where my sister was arranging furniture!"

"Sister, you say?"

"Angela."

"Sweet tooth?"

"Definitely."

"Then there could be—double rations of marmalade?"

"She might be willing to oblige."

"You'd bring some and she'd bring some, is that the prospect we're looking at?"

"Yes, certainly."

"Well, then I'll just fade back into the furniture. You leave the ration at the head of the stairs."

"Of course, but come along and meet Angela." Adrian ran ahead toward Angela's alcove. For a moment he saw something resembling a tree stump hurrying off, and then a cat's tail disappearing. "Angela," he said, as he rushed into the alcove, "I want you to meet—"

He turned, and Angela turned with him, but all she saw was a little puff of dust at the end of the corridor, where Pinover had scurried away.

On the following day, Angela and Adrian rounded up poached egg, toast, some dried salty fish that tasted like crackers, a pot of tea, and a large tin of marmalade. And while Cook was having her nap, they snuck into the attic and carried the food over to Angela's cozy little corner.

"Well," said Adrian, "should we ring a gong or something?"

"I guess, before the egg gets cold."

A gong was close by, hanging between a pair of polished buffalo horns. Adrian gave it a good whack but only the cat came out. It began to sniff the fish dish. Angela gave him some, and a saucer of cream. "But," she said, "where's Ginger?"

"And Mr. Pinover," said Adrian. "He wouldn't miss out on marmalade, not for anything."

"Do you think something's happened?"

"I shouldn't doubt it," said Adrian. "We'd best go after them."

"All right," said Angela, "but don't be beastly," by which she meant spiders.

They went down the central artery of the attic, between enormous stacks of books and magazines, as well as piles of foot stools, kitchen chairs, and coat racks.

"H . . . e . . . lll . . . pppp," came a voice.

"That's Ginger!" said Angela.

They hurried along, and found the poor woman wedged in a hip bath. "Oh, that Pinover," she said, as they pulled her out. "He's supposed to keep things in order. But look at how he's let it pile up. Umbrella stands and wash basins next to billiard balls—that's what I slipped on, you see, a billiard ball. And went tumbling." She looked at Angela. "Did you bring the cat his breakfast of toast, dried fish, poached egg, and tea?"

"Yes," said Angela. "And he loved it."

"*All* of it?"

"Oh no, there's lots left over."

"Who's this?" asked Ginger, casting a suspicious glance at Adrian.

"My brother."

"Make a nice tree stump. Well, let's go find that old fool, Pinover. He should have been here by now."

"Do you often meet him?" asked Angela.

"Not if I can help it. But the stuffed tiger is loose."

"Tiger!" Adrian's eyes lit with excitement. Conveniently a pith helmet was on a nearby hat rack, and popping it on he felt much more the part. "Now, I'm ready!"

"You're ready, all right," said Ginger and gave Angela a look, which Angela returned, concerning the usefulness of brothers.

"Pinover, where are you!" called Ginger, but not too loudly, for the tiger, she said, could be anywhere.

They moved along slowly, Ginger leading the way, past a pile of bathtubs of every possible kind, and a stack of bicycle wheels, and a wall of dishes, enough to supply a hotel.

"If I see the tiger," said Adrian, "I shall wrestle it into submission."

"Is he always like this?" asked Ginger.

"Frequently," said Angela.

"What ho!" cried Pinover, leaping out in front of them and brandishing an ancient musket. He wore a safari outfit and had an enormous amount of gear attached to his belt, including a gas mask.

"You old fool," said Ginger. "Have you set the trap?"

"Of course I have," said Pinover. He flashed a keen glance at Adrian. "Marmalade?"

"Back there," said Adrian, pointing in the direction from which they'd come.

"Well, I'll just be a moment," said Pinover, and made a move to get it, but Ginger hooked him around the neck with her umbrella handle.

"This is not the time for marmalade."

"I'll be the judge of that," said Pinover, scrambling free. "Marmalade's what you need when chasing a tiger." But he fell into step with Ginger, and they moved deeper into the attic.

"It's your fault he's loose," said Ginger.

"Oh, it is, is it," grumbled Pinover.

A blood-chilling roar stopped everyone—the very walls of the attic shook with the sound. The hair on the back of Angela's neck certainly stood on end, and it was all Adrian could do to keep from diving under a pile of sofas.

"It's coming from there," said Pinover, pointing his musket toward a shadowy line of hinged Chinese screens far ahead of them.

"Where did you set the trap?" asked Ginger.

"Let me just . . . check the map." Pinover pulled it out, studied it thoughtfully. " . . . I marked it . . . with an X . . . odd I can't make it out." He looked up from the map. "It's been tampered with."

"Children," said Ginger, "you'd better go back downstairs."

"Oh, we couldn't leave you to face the tiger alone," said Angela.

"This map," said Pinover, folding it up, "has been of enormous value to us once again."

Again the roar sounded, and Angela saw a shadow moving behind the screens. "There!"

"Yes, that's him," said Pinover. "We've got to take the high ground." Pinover helped Ginger up onto a set of bureau drawers, and the little lady climbed on from there, with the others behind her, up a high wall of furniture.

"She climbs well, doesn't she," said Pinover. "You wouldn't think she'd be that spry."

"Shut your lip," said Ginger. They all crowded in beside her, on the edge of a coffee table balanced at the top of the pile. Pinover raised his binoculars but dropped his musket, which hit the floor and went off, blowing a hole in Ginger's umbrella and very nearly killing everyone.

"Of all the stupid things—" Ginger held up her shattered umbrella.

"Plenty more where that came from," said Pinover. "I've learned never to regret anything lost or exploded up here."

"There's the tiger!" Adrian pointed, to the edge of the screens, where the beast was poking its head out, eyes brightly shining.

"Glass," said Pinover, "and they're as sharp as can be."

"But how can a stuffed tiger walk around?" asked Angela.

"It's one of life's little mysteries," said Pinover.

"Oh do shut up, Pinover," said Ginger.

The tiger lifted its head, and its burning gaze fell upon the little group. Its large red tongue came out and it licked its lips.

"Hungry," said Pinover.

"What does it eat?" asked Adrian.

"Stuffing."

"Stuffing?"

"Makes an awful mess. Can ruin an acre of hassocks in no time flat. Chews them all up, you see." Pinover raised his binoculars. "All right, I've got the marmalade in view. Big tin of it." He lowered the binoculars and turned to Adrian. "It'll be a job to get to it now, with that dumb beast in the road."

The tiger was now at the foot of the pile of furniture, growling in a most frightening way. "Can it climb?"asked Angela.

"Climb? I should say so," said Pinover.

"Now don't frighten the girl, Pinover," said Ginger.

"Well, she should know the bitter truth."

The tiger gazed up at them, a fierce look in its glass eyes. It opened its jaws, and yellow teeth gleamed, as it let out a horrible roar. Then it proceeded to reach up and tear the stuffing out of a nice little love seat. The entire pile on which the group sat began to sway.

"We're going to be toppled!" cried Ginger.

"I'll go down," said Adrian, "and wrestle it into submission."

Pinover held Adrian by the strap of his pith helmet. "I'll go first, laddie. I've dealt with the fiend before." Pinover started down the tower of furniture, from bedpost to bureau drawer to writing table. The tiger watched him out of the corner of its eye, as it continued to rip out stuffing and swallow it down. Pinover stopped, just out of reach of the beast.

"G'wan, you ugly devil . . ." He waved his gas mask at the creature.

Adrian could hold back no longer. He leapt from where he was, down into the aisle beside the tiger. The animal whipped quickly around, snarling. Its long claws missed Adrian by a hair. But now Angela, who couldn't allow her brother to face so much danger alone, was in back of the tiger. "Leave . . . him . . . alone!" she shouted, and gave the tiger's tail such a terrible yank the thing came off in her hand.

The tiger roared in anger and Angela ran, tail in hand, toward the Chinese screens, with the tiger leaping after her. "I'm sorry," she cried, "I didn't mean to pull so hard."

The tiger did not accept her apology, tigers rarely do. It roared again, and snapped its jaws at her, just missing the edge of her skirt.

"What ho! What ho!" The voice of Pinover came to Angela as she ducked behind the screens, and then Adrian shouted, "I'll wrestle the beast into submission, see if I won't!"

"Tiger would have caught her by now," said Pinover, as he and Adrian gave chase, "except it made a pig of itself on stuffing. Stuffed with the stuff, you see. Lucky for the young lady."

Ginger was making her way down the tower of furniture, handbag in one hand, her exploded umbrella in the other. "Pinover!" she shouted. "Attract the beast's attention!"

"What ho!" called Pinover, but his energy was gone. He sagged against one of the screens. "Marmalade would have made the difference. You'd have seen me sprinting."

"I've never seen you do anything but get lost and cause trouble." Ginger straightened her hat.

"A few deep breaths," said Pinover, filling his lungs. "Now I'm fit."

"You'll never be fit."

Pinover, Ginger, and Adrian hurried off again, up the aisle, past a tower of marble sinks, a wall of doll carriages of every size and shape, and a jumble of old radios. Far in the distance, Angela made a quick leap to the left through a stack of several hundred pairs of shoes, and Pinover pointed into a small nearby aisle. "This way! I know a shortcut—"

"Shortcut," grumbled Ginger, scurrying along behind him, her little legs working hard. "People could be lost for years following your shortcuts."

"Will the tiger—eat Angela?" asked Adrian, gulping hard.

"Well, it prefers stuffing," said Pinover. "But it's irritated, you see, regarding the yanked-off tail. Remarkable the way it came off. Your sister has a grip like a gorilla. Probably had marmalade for breakfast, am I right?"

"You and your marmalade," said Ginger, who was completely winded now, and extremely red in the face. "If you hadn't wakened the tiger up in the first place—"

"I was tiptoeing past it."

"You were blowing a bugle."

Pinover blushed. "It is the rare person who, finding a bugle, doesn't want to give it a blow."

"Not next to a sleeping stuffed tiger. No sane person would do a thing like that." Ginger bent suddenly over, hand to her side. "I've got a stitch from all this running around."

"Breathe deeply."

"Shut your yap."

"Only trying to help."

Adrian took Ginger by the arm. "Are you all right?"

"Never mind about me." Ginger poked Pinover in the back with her exploded umbrella. "Get going."

"I'm consulting the map." Pinover had it out, was studying it carefully. "Yes, right, just as I thought—" Holding it in his hand, he pointed the way; they took three steps forward and a huge cage fell down around them, slamming shut on all sides.

"Found the trap," said Pinover.

"You sawed-off turnip," said Ginger, her fingers wrapped around the bars. "Look at the fix you and your map have got us in now."

Adrian rattled the bars, then took a flying run at them, and bounced off, seeing stars.

"It's a fine trap," said Pinover, "one of the best, I should say, though of course I'm no expert." He paced around its edges, and pointed out the firmness of its joints. "Hold an elephant, it would."

"First he wakes the tiger up, then he catches us in the tiger trap, and now he talks about elephants."

Ginger swung her handbag at Pinover but he was too fast for her.

Adrian stared out of the cage. In the distance the tiger was roaring. "Angela!" he called. "I'm coming! Hang on!"

"Adrian!" Angela's voice came closer. "Adrian!" She appeared, on the run, swinging the tiger's tail. The tiger was loping along behind her.

"We're caged, Angela!" shouted Adrian.

"A lot of good that does me," said Angela, and then she was on by, down the aisle, heading toward the old radios.

"Throw away the tail!" called Ginger.

Angela hadn't even realized she had it in her hand until this moment. She flung it behind her, and the stuffed tiger stopped, and gazed down at it wistfully. Then it lifted its head and turned toward Ginger, in the cage.

"Pick it up and bring it here," said Ginger, sternly.

The tiger picked the tail up in its mouth gently and came toward the cage.

"Now that's a remarkable sight," said Pinover.

"Don't move," said Ginger. "If you move, I'll clout you one."

"I'm frozen in place," said Pinover. "I'm as still as a stuffed owl."

They watched as the tiger came slowly, tail in its jaws, and stood in front of Ginger.

Ginger took the tail from the tiger's mouth. "Well—turn around," she ordered sharply, and the tiger did.

Adrian started to move closer, but Pinover grabbed him by the shirt. "She'll clout you."

Ginger opened her handbag and took out needle and thread. "This might sting a bit," she said to the tiger, "but that's what you get for running around chasing people."

Angela peeked over the old radios. "Is it safe?"

"Not yet, dear," said Ginger, threading the needle. "Now," she said to the tiger, "you hold still."

The tiger closed its eyes and gritted its teeth as Ginger sewed its tail back on. "You're just a big overgrown pussycat, aren't you," said Ginger soothingly. She turned to Adrian. "Come over here, young man, and pet the tiger."

Adrian did so, scratching the tiger's stripes. "Oh," said Adrian, "it's wonderful to pet a tiger." Angela, seeing how much Adrian was enjoying it, came forward to join in, but the tiger opened its eyes and made a low, growling sound. It had *not* forgotten who'd yanked its tail off.

"I'm sorry," said Angela, and held out a handful of stuffing for the tiger to nibble on. "Please forgive me, but you were trying to eat my brother."

The tiger eyed her suspiciously, but could not resist the stuffing, which had come from a very expensive couch cushion.

"We have here," said Pinover, "a remarkable display of communication between man and beast."

"There," said Ginger, "that's not going to come off again in a hurry." She broke the thread, made a nice little knot under the tiger's tail, which didn't show at all. The tiger turned around, looked at its tail, tried it out a few times and saw that it rotated, went up and down, and moved from side to side. It was purring now, a deep rumbling sound, and when Ginger put her hand out, the tiger licked it with its big rough tongue. It licked Adrian's hand. It might have licked Angela's hand too, but Ginger advised against finding out. "Just stay behind the radios until it goes away."

"But will anybody be safe up here ever again?" asked Adrian.

"Well, it's stuffed with stuffing," said Ginger, "and it's going to get sleepy pretty soon. And a stuffed tiger will sleep for years unless—" She cast a sharp glance at Pinover. "—somebody wakes it with a bugle."

"I'm all done bugling," said Pinover.

"That remains to be seen," said Ginger.

"There goes the tiger," said Adrian.

They watched it moving slowly away, past the radios and the doll carriages, and on deeper into the long shadows of the jumbled corridor. Angela crept out from behind the radios.

"Find us a saw, will you," said Pinover, "that's a good girl."

Angela found one just a few feet away, and they all took turns sawing at the bars of the cage. "How sweet is freedom," said Pinover, as the bars fell apart.

Ginger, Adrian, and Pinover stepped out of the cage. "Now," said Pinover, "marmalade." He pulled out his map, studied it, and pointed. "Should be straight in that direction."

"It's this way," said Ginger, and marched everyone off in precisely the opposite direction.

"Gifted with a natural homing sense," said Pinover. "Just like a pigeon." He followed along behind the group, checking his map and compass and shaking his head.

They found the marmalade, and had a lovely little tea in Angela's area, and Mr. Pinover told of the time the stuffed alligator woke in the attic, owing, said Ginger, to a certain someone in a gaudy marching uniform going around beating on a bass drum all morning long.

"Adrian, look at the time," said Angela. "Cook'll be waking."

"We've got to go," said Adrian. "But we'll be back tomorrow. With marmalade."

Angela and Adrian went down the stairs, and out through the attic door, into the upstairs hallway. "It seems so short and narrow," said Angela.

"Yes," said Adrian, "no corridors, no aisles of furniture, no tiger."

Cook's door opened. "Well, what've you been up to? No good, I'm sure." She rubbed her eyes. "I had the most awful nap. Kept hearing roaring and growling."

"It was probably something you ate," said Adrian. "Maybe you had too much marmalade."

"Don't be smart with me, young man."

"Sorry," said Adrian.

"Don't mind him, Cook," said Angela. "He's been in a cage."

"It's where he belongs." Cook went off grumbling,

and Adrian and Angela tried to adjust to the narrow corridors and the tiny rooms.

"I used to think our house was big," said Angela.

"The attic's the big place. People don't know. They ought to go up and look some time."

"Well, they'll get an awful shock," said Angela.

That night at supper, Adrian asked his father, "Did you ever know anyone named Pinover?"

"And Ginger?" asked Angela.

Their father looked up sharply from his soup, as if waking from a dream. He seemed to remember something very old and very important; his spoon remained poised in the air and a faraway look came into his eyes. But then slowly a cloud covered them, and he lowered his spoon into his soup. "Can't say that I have. For a moment there—but no, I've never met anyone by those names."

Later, when supper was over, and Adrian and Angela were alone, Adrian said, "Well, *I'll* never forget Mr. Pinover and Ginger."

"Nor I," said Angela, "ever, ever, ever."

"He shall always have his marmalade."

"And she shall always have her toast and tea."

"Oh promise, Angela, if you ever see me forgetting, you'll give me a pinch."

"And you do the same for me."

And they shook hands on it. But when they went up the attic on the following day, it was just a small, shabby place they found, with a few boxes, some old chairs, and a stack of magazines.

"Mr. Pinover!" cried Adrian.

"Ginger!" called Angela.

The attic was silent. No one was there at all. But then, over in a corner, Adrian found— "The map!" He opened it up on the floor in front of them and saw, scrawled across the top in big wriggly letters,

Pinover's Map of the World
Guaranteed Absolutely Accurate

Afterword

And so ends The Empty Notebook. There were more stories to it, I'm sure, but dawn had come to my uncle's room, the fire was dead in the grate, and the enchantment was over; I was staring at a blank page, and no further trace of the mysterious blue lettering was visible. I laid down my Uncle's pen, and made my way downstairs. It was early but my cousin was already at the breakfast table. "Well," he said, gazing up from his toast, "you look as if you haven't slept a wink."

"I haven't," I said, and almost began to tell him what was in the notebook that I'd tucked under my arm. But something in his gaze, some bland assurance about the way things are in this life, discouraged me and I remained silent.

Tales From the Empty Notebook

"Taking one of the empty notebooks?" he asked, as he poured me tea. "You're welcome to it, of course. I can always replace it with another, equally empty," He laughed, and it wasn't a cruel laugh, merely an unconscious one. I stared out the window toward the garden; the green lawn sparkled in the first rays of the morning sun, and Uncle's spirit still clung to me, yet I could feel it evaporating, like the dew from the grass. I promised myself that I should return again some other night, in hopes that more pages of his notebook would be revealed to me. I have not done so, for the affairs of the world have lured me on to other things, as the world will do whenever we come near that realm which is meant to be hidden from our eyes. Such secrets are apparently closely guarded, and numerous obstacles have come into my path, some petty, and some formidable, and all of them keeping me from the simple trip to my uncle's house and another night at his desk. Yet my promise re-mains, and in time, perhaps, it will be fulfilled.